SIGN LANGUAGES

SIGN LANGUAGES

Stories by
JAMES HANNAH

UNIVERSITY OF MISSOURI PRESS

Columbia and London

Copyright © 1993 by James Hannah
University of Missouri Press, Columbia, Missouri 65201
Printed and bound in the United States of America
All rights reserved
5 4 3 2 1   97 96 95 94 93

Library of Congress Cataloging-in-Publication Data

Hannah, James, 1951–
    Sign languages / James Hannah.
       p. cm.
    ISBN 0-8262-0900-9 (alk. paper)
    I. Title.
    PS3558.A4762S54   1993
    813'.54—dc20   93-12820
                                                                                 CIP

∞™ This paper meets the requirements of the American National Standard for Permanence of Paper for Printed Library Materials, Z39.48, 1984.

Designer: Rhonda Miller
Typesetter: Connell-Zeko Type & Graphics
Printer and binder: Thomson-Shore, Inc.
Typefaces: Palacio and Eras

Some of the stories in this volume appeared originally in *Descant* ("Residue"), *Kansas Quarterly* ("Emollients"), *Llano Estacado* ("Interstate"), *New Growth: Contemporary Short Stories by Texas Writers* ("Friends of Beccari"), *River City Review* ("Sign Language"), and *South Carolina Review* ("Gypsy Moth").
    The author also wishes to thank the National Endowment for the Arts for its financial assistance.

To
My father and brother

In memory of
Suzanne Comer

CONTENTS

INTERSTATE   1

EMOLLIENTS   13

RESIDUE   33

HISTOIRE DE MON TEMPS   44

FRIENDS OF BECCARI   61

BACKYARDS   78

GYPSY MOTH   101

RISING WATER,
WIND-DRIVEN RAIN   112

SIGN LANGUAGE   135

SIGN LANGUAGES

INTERSTATE

Henry was exhausted. He had driven from Cincinnati through Kentucky and Tennessee, and now they passed to the west of Memphis. He rubbed his eyes with a knuckle and slowed the pickup. The interstate traffic mixed with crosstown drivers.

In the seat next to him his six-year-old daughter, Maggie, played one of her tapes full of high-pitched voices and irritating tunes she sang along with under her breath.

Just a few minutes ago, for the sixth or seventh time since they'd left home at sunrise, he had explained to her how they'd stay in a motel tonight and tomorrow they would arrive at his parents' in Dallas.

"And you'll leave me and the houseplants at Grandmommie's, go down to Austin, rent us a nice place until next spring when you and Mommie can find one to buy, and fly back and bring Mommie and brother down in the new car. Then the whole family will come up to get me and the ferns, right?" She had beamed at him because she remembered it all.

Now he glanced at her face, long and narrow like her mother's, and her eyes, which were the dark blue of very clear, deep water. The color often reminded him of a trip he and Martha had taken to the Bahamas years ago before the two children and all the other things that happen.

Earlier he and Maggie had sung songs. They had talked about the colors of cars and trucks, played "I Spy." She had napped, eaten a lot. The floorboard was full of bottles and candy wrappers and McDonald's bags. Henry worried she'd get sick and want her mother.

But she hadn't gotten ill or even whined much, and Henry had thanked God a dozen times already. He'd never been on a trip alone with her where she didn't have at least her brother to fight with and talk to. He considered the fact that he didn't know her very well.

All he wanted was for her not to make any trouble. To be still and quiet, to nap when she needed to, and to keep well covered with the old soft quilt they'd brought. The blast of cold from the air-conditioner was all that kept him awake now.

He needed to try to think about everything. But he knew the driving was becoming dangerously easy and automatic. He had no reflexes left. They sped on at seventy-five. His exhausted mind was a tangle of projections about the future mixed with the past that would be Cincinnati soon. He knew how fearful he could be and so had that to combat. And now a lane change or a swerve to avoid a jolting hole in the concrete muddled it all.

He had spent three weeks at the Austin office in February. And Janet had come to his hotel room for dinner. They had eaten awful Mexican food and drunk good margaritas and talked about nothing much and that was all there was to it.

But since then he'd known that would not always be all unless he said it would. He had never before been interested in anyone else, but now he knew he was because despite all the worry about Maggie, about the move, and his insecurity and Martha's loss of a good job, he tried not to think about the innocuous dinner. About how anything more would change everything at home.

His eyes, even behind the prescription shades, felt needled from the thick summer haze complicated by the dusty harvesting of fields of winter wheat. And, in places, the remaining fields of stubble were burning in black and orange rows. It was all desolation. He thought of his father who, as a young man, had walked out of Burma with "Vinegar Joe" Stilwell. "Desolation," his father'd say, a man with almost no words for anybody.

Henry recalled a book about Stilwell he'd checked out of the library when he first entered college. Now he tried to remember the photographs of the chaos of escape. Smoldering villages; looting; huddled, frightened people. Bodies against the flimsy walls of huts. Stilwell was in most of the photographs, teeth clenched around his pipe. And behind him a line of emaciated men in tattered uniforms. Any one of them could have been his father; he couldn't tell, though he had bent close, angling the glossy paper away from the light. They were hurrying through that countryside toward India.

The farmers had already burned everything here as far as he could see. He put the back of his hand to the windshield, and the June heat leached through. The setting sun was in his eyes now. He adjusted the visor, but he could see only the car immediately in front of him. He shifted his weight and noticed Maggie had fallen asleep again. Reaching over, he covered her, raked some cookie crumbs to the floor, and switched off the tape player.

He left the pickup running at a roadside park while he tried to defecate. When he returned, Maggie was still asleep. He thought he shouldn't have left her. And he recalled how once, with David, he'd gone into a 7-Eleven and locked him in the car with the keys. He'd had to pretend calm and point with a steady finger at the door latch and motion for him to pull it up. But he'd laughed a toothless grin, and finally Henry had had to call the police.

At five-thirty he tried to listen to the NPR news on the radio. Something tremendous had happened somewhere far away. He kept adjusting the dial, but they were not close enough to Little Rock for a clear, strong signal.

Instead they listened to music from quickly fading local stations and played a game she thought of. Actually only she played; he refereed. She'd listen to a few lines and tell him if it was a happy song or a sad one. He was surprised at how good she did, though when there was only music she had more difficulty.

"I'm really tired."

"I'll bet you are," she nodded.

Henry heard Martha in her intonation. "I really am," he said and was embarrassed at trying to convince Maggie he was telling the truth.

"I'll bet so."

"Are you okay? Tired too?" He thought her mother read to her every night and sometimes rocked her to sleep. He also knew Maggie often slept with her brother and wondered if they should get one bed or two that evening. He was afraid she would miss her mother and wouldn't be able to get to sleep in a strange room.

"Yep, me too."

"And remember, tomorrow you'll be at Grandmommie's house. That's something to think about, isn't it?" He watched her smile and nod vigorously, and he was relieved.

Just at sunset, on the other side of Little Rock, they pulled into the Mid-Arkansan Inn. Their room was on the second level a distance from the stairs. Pulling back the curtains, he could barely see the top of the pickup and, across the vast and empty parking lot, Chuck's Best Steak House. The woman at the desk had given him two ten-percent-off coupons for dinner and the breakfast buffet. Though it was after eight, the place looked closed.

Henry had dragged up their two suitcases and now lay on the bed farthest from the window, his eyes closed to the standard decor of a room under fifty dollars. Maybe I won't do this thing with Janet, he thought. Then he considered managing an entire branch office. There'd be travel all over the southwest region. And though he was sure he appeared confident to others in the business, he knew exactly how deep all that went. He had always had to work harder, longer hours just to keep up.

He listened to Maggie unpack her suitcase and arrange her bed. She sang under her breath. Once she whispered to her dolls and whistled a single clear note of surprise. He opened his eyes and turned on his side; his back was a complication of aches and dull dead spots he massaged with cramped fingers. He felt the sway of the pickup.

"Well, I'll fill the ice bucket," Maggie said as she tore off the plastic wrap.

"I don't think we need it, you know. Nothing to drink. We'll go over and eat in a few minutes, okay?" And Henry lay back. He and Martha had both wanted David, and David had outdistanced his attention. By the time this blue-eyed child had appeared, he had turned back to work for many reasons. It had been like college, where he learned he had to study hard without the interruption of companions. Maggie had come as Martha's child and joined up with David. He figured it was just the way things work and thought it might have been different if they'd both been boys.

"We always get ice. That's my job, Dad. Brother finds the TV programs and helps me unpack, and Mom *oversees* us."

"Do you need help unpacking?"

"Oh no, see."

Henry propped his head on his hand to watch her open the bureau drawers.

"It's all done. And I put your stuff in the bathroom." She nodded and closed the drawers. "Be back in a minute."

"Hey, wait." Henry sat up slowly and straightened his twisted clothes. "I'll go with you."

"Nope, I am *six* now. It's back around the corner. We passed it, remember? You can watch me from the door if you want to."

She wore shorts, and he watched her strong legs and hips. Her back was perfectly straight like the backs of women he'd seen riding English style. The parking lot of the motel was filling with late arrivals off the interstate. Two noisy older couples walked slowly between rows of parked cars toward Chuck's Best Steak House. Lightning reddened the bottoms of distant thunderheads.

Before he'd met Martha and before he'd turned to studying so hard there had been a girl named Alice. Alice Williams.

She'd flown to Los Angeles on a special flight full of pregnant women and gotten an abortion. Now the cost seemed small—a car payment or two—but then it had set him back for months. He'd seen her once afterward. Now he remembered why he'd been unable to say no to Martha about this one. Though he had known it was foolish, he had believed for a long time he must do penance for the abortion. That he must pay back that thin, awkward girl. Thunder crackled in the distance, and Henry thought Maggie should have returned by now. He left the door open behind him.

"Maggie? Maggie?" He hurried along the concrete balcony, but Maggie came racing around the corner giggling, her face red. The hollow tubular ice tumbled from the bucket and skittered through the iron railings.

Henry ate slowly, letting the food soothe him. The steak was better than average. Across from him the table was littered with the jumbled debris of Maggie's meal.

"Wow, I'm tight as a tick," she said.

Henry nodded, recognizing a phrase his father had taught her. She had quickly devoured all of a chopped sirloin sandwich and a slice of cherry cheesecake. Then, finding he had access to a confused but huge salad bar complete with ice cream and the makings for exotic sundaes, she had eaten a half-dozen other things as well.

Henry took more iced tea from the waitress and couldn't tell if her face was smiling at the child's excess or scowling at his obvious lack of control. "Thanks."

The waitress ducked her head and hurried off to her corner to resume a long brown cigarette. The only other customers were a trucker whose rig idled under the motel sign and a woman young enough to be his daughter. Her bare left shoulder was a patchwork of dark tattoos over her pale redhead's skin. Her hand, under the table, was in the man's khaki pants. They laughed and talked quietly. Henry wondered if they'd known each other for a long time, or if they'd met down the road somewhere when she'd asked for a ride or he'd been kind enough to stop.

Just as Henry finished eating, a thunderstorm rolled over them, rattling the stacks of tea glasses and causing the lights to flicker. The rain came down in heavy sheets, obscuring the parked truck, blurring the red, white, and blue neon of the motel sign.

"Wow . . . boom . . . bet Mom and Brother are scared, huh? Bet they wish they were here." Maggie wet her finger and lifted bacon bits from the edge of his salad. "Hey! We could have gone swimming. Mom packed the suits!" She looked up, her blue eyes suddenly sad.

Henry nodded. "We got in too late. Grandmommie'll take you to the pool. Remember there's one right down the street in the park? You've been . . . but you don't remember it, do you?" He was afraid that now with the dark and the loud storm and the strange bed coming up she might think too much of Martha and home. He was afraid she'd cry and he wouldn't be able to console her. He recalled some truly awful night in a motel room in Wisconsin when David was nine months old. Looking out into the rain at the watery headlights of cars still on the interstate, he thought about how much things were going to change in less than a month. Soon their furniture would move past this café and over the exchange and west to Texas. He pictured himself and his family in the back of the van doing their usual stuff—watching TV or cooking dinner.

They lingered, waiting for the rain to diminish, until the waitress asked them to leave. She had another job somewhere else. They took a newspaper from the tiny vestibule and made a dash through the downpour that had brought a hot blanket of steam up from the concrete.

In the room, Henry toweled off their hair and prepared Maggie's toothbrush. She brushed methodically. He wanted to hurry her but didn't.

"Hey, let's phone Mom and Brother and tell 'em about that cheesecake and sundae bar. Brother'll be mad as a wet hen."

Maggie laughed. "That's like us running across the parking lot. Two wet hens."

"They're at camp, remember?"

"Oh yeah, that's right. I'm being silly now."

Henry put her wet clothes over the shower curtain and dried her hair more thoroughly against the chill of the room.

"It's past eleven. You should have been asleep hours ago. What would your . . ." He bit his lip and gave her a kiss as she settled into the bed near the window.

"Can I color some?"

"Oh Maggie, aren't you exhausted?"

"Nope, not a bit."

"I shouldn't have let you have a Coke."

"Well, you did. And now I'll just have to color."

"For a minute."

"For two minutes."

"Two minutes and that's all."

She jumped down to her huge canvas bag of toys and brought out a cigar box of crayons and a thick coloring book.

In the bathroom Henry could hear the rain better. He undressed and washed his face. Though he was all aches, he decided to shower in the morning. If he closed his eyes he saw the interstate ahead and the desolation of flaring fields. The sky was dust and smoke. He thought about his father. He was two different men. One a starving young soldier forcing himself to keep up, to stay on the narrow roads leading from the fields into the more dangerous jungle. The other they'd see tomorrow morning standing behind the screen door. He'd wave brusquely with his left hand and fumble with the latch, mumbling to himself about the conspiracy of all things that stick or come loose.

He thought about Janet; saw her long thin arm on the back of the couch. Martha had never worn nail polish, and he had never asked her to. The memory of its dazzle further pained his eyes.

He put on his pajama bottoms and turned out all the lights

except the dim one over Maggie's shoulder. Her head was down, her hand busy.

Henry read the HBO guide and found that a movie he had wanted to see for years had started less than fifteen minutes earlier. He rolled the TV stand as far as it would go and turned its back to Maggie.

"Not for kids, huh?" she said.

"Right. And you need to go to bed now."

"I'm in bed," she giggled.

"To sleep. You know what I mean." But he kept his voice light.

The movie was about alien things like long worms with terrible eyes and teeth. They crawled down throats and became people. You had to catch them in the dark when they became disoriented or something. Henry couldn't understand it all, though he couldn't believe missing fifteen minutes was the reason.

The movie was truly violent, and he kept glancing at Maggie and turning down the volume when they emerged to claim new victims and turning it up when the good guy, a small-town doctor, was begging people to believe him, that he had the answers.

"Oh God, not them, they're ones too?" Henry spoke softly.

Near the end there was the butchery he expected in a movie where the violence is done to aliens that only look like people. When the credits came on, Henry remembered where he was and slowly turned his head to look at Maggie. But she wasn't asleep, though she hadn't made a sound in over an hour. She was staring at him, her face half in shadow, the eye in the lighted half bright and moist.

"What is it? Maggie, what's wrong?"

He switched off the TV but still sat on the edge of his bed.

"I have a funny feeling."

"Is it your stomach? Do you need to potty?"

She shook her head, but her eye didn't leave his face.

"What is it?"

"I think something really bad is going to happen to us."

Henry didn't move. He knew exactly what he should do and say, but he didn't move or speak. Then he knelt, his hands on her hands. "What do you think it is? Is it about the trip? Or later . . . in Texas? Is it my job? Or Mommie or David? What is it, Maggie?" He clenched her hands and shook them. He thought maybe she knew because she was a child. He had never been superstitious before but now he was filled with it. He squeezed her hands harder and they stared at one another.

"I don't know," she whispered. "It's just this feeling I've had. Something terrible is going to happen to all of us."

She began to cry and pulled out of his weakened grasp. "I want my mother!" she shouted and flung herself to the other side of the bed.

Henry went to the bathroom and wet a hand towel. He wiped his face, but the cold water was lukewarm. He looked at himself without turning on the mirror light. He had never felt more exhausted.

He calmed Maggie by wiping her face and neck and chest. The crying and hours of travel caused her to drop off to sleep once he held her in his lap, his aching back against the flimsy headboard.

It was after one in the morning when he switched off the light and lay in his own bed. But he slept erratically. Though he turned the thermostat up, the fan continued to blow frigid air. Frequently he got up and made sure Maggie was covered.

Minutes before the six o'clock wake-up call, he sat up in bed. In the dream just now he had felt his large hands on the child's. But somehow that wasn't what he'd pictured. Or this part had come earlier. He had been coming up some stairs and, as he stepped onto the landing, he saw an old woman on a wooden bench waiting outside a frosted glass door. She was dressed in dark colors, long out of fashion, a flat hat on her head, her face turned away from him. Her bluish hair spilled from around her hat; she tapped anxiously on the back of the bench.

He was sure it was Maggie, and he knew, if it were true, he

had been dead for a very long time. That if he were remembered at all it was there somewhere behind her graceful finger's rhythmic tapping.

Maggie sang under her breath as she took a bath and then dressed and carefully folded her clothes back into her suitcase. Henry raked his stuff into his overnight bag and left her in order to pay the bill. Outside, the sun lay like a huge deformed yolk on the tree line across the interstate. The humidity was almost unbearable; his earlier shower seemed useless.

By seven they had repacked the pickup and Henry had inspected the wilting plants. He checked the oil and dripped some from the dipstick onto his fresh khakis. "Dammit to hell."

"Shame on you, naughty boy." Maggie spoke to him for the first time since waking, but he didn't look over the motor at her. She turned away and sat in the opened door and began singing to Mr. Pete, the ragged, lanky monkey that had once been David's.

Chuck's Best Steak House was busy, filled with city employees and state road crews jostling one another, smoking early cigarettes that choked Henry as they sat.

"Wow! Look at that buffet." Maggie turned on her knees in the booth and waved her hands.

Henry reached out and took her left arm and pulled her across the table, almost tipping the glasses of ice water. "What's this?" The tan back of her arm was mottled; the bruise almost encircled her wrist, more vivid on the pale underside. Look what I've done, he thought. Look at this. Immediately he lightened his grip, his hand barely touching her forearm.

"Oh, I fell off Brother's bicycle. Remember? It was the last day of school, I think." She shrugged and smiled at him. "Let's eat."

"But not so much. Not like yesterday, okay?"

Maggie turned and sat down hard on the vinyl. "It was *fun*."

Henry opened his menu. The photographs were too bright and sharp. Brilliant yellow eggs. Crimson rashers of bacon.

"I think that's what made you unhappy last night . . . all that food . . . candy, hamburgers, chips, Cokes . . . your mother wouldn't like it." He closed the menu. "We'll have some cereal, okay?"

Maggie rubbed her arm. "Food didn't cause it. It wasn't my stomach."

"Listen, nothing's going to happen to us. It was all that food and riding in the pickup all day and the heat." He reached for her hands, but they darted under the table.

He took up his iced water. The outside of it was slippery from condensation. "You don't know what it is, now do you?" He bent his head and looked into her dark blue eyes that held his own. "No, of course you don't. Because it was just the travel and the upcoming move." Henry nodded. "Nothing'll happen. I'm your daddy and I solemnly declare that." He heard his own voice and he lowered it, made it gruff like a cartoon character, a cartoon bear, and her eyes shifted to his lips and then she laughed and squirmed in her seat.

They ordered and ate their cereal and halved a sausage patty. He drank the rest of her milk and wiped his mouth.

"I'm sorry . . ." Henry said as he dipped the edge of his napkin in the cold water and removed flecks of cereal from her chin. "I'm sorry about last night." But Maggie was twisting with energy and fussing with the monkey. "Let's get going, Mr. Pete. Grandmommie is waiting with open arms. She's got a candle burning in the window, Mr. Pete."

They settled themselves in the pickup. Henry drove over the overpass and turned onto the access ramp. He tried keeping his thoughts on the traffic as he accelerated to seventy. The sun was behind them, and he hoped they'd reach Dallas before it arched overhead and turned the road to pewter and addled his brain. Right now he pictured his father in a meticulous dress uniform, as lanky as Mr. Pete. He would have some trouble coming down the front steps, but he had once walked at Stilwell's side right out of Burma.

EMOLLIENTS

Her chapped hands, dipped in the lavatory, turned the water pink. "Jesus," she said, and held them there as she looked at herself in the unlighted mirror. Pushing her nose close to the cool glass, she turned her head. Where has the wind harmed me? she asked, and looked at lips, temples, cheeks. I am beautiful, she said with her eyes at their reflection.

And she is telling the truth.

But just in case, she applied a half-dozen oils and lotions. The consistency of Todd's semen, she thought. Warming it on her fingertips, she glistened eyelids and chin. She perused her olive face. I'm half Indian, she told them all at work and before in college and on down to when she had found out. On your mother's side, her mother had said. Because her father was pale, always twenty-eight, and in uniform in the photograph on the chest of drawers in the pink light of her girl's room. And now here, on the other side of this very wall.

She saw, as she rubbed her warming dark skin, the pores healthy and small-grained like the finest paper at work where she was immensely popular. The men took her to lunch, the women did too, or she treated them. There were no hard feelings; they were all the same age. Everyone in the office was. And so were the clients she opened up houses for or office fronts in strip malls.

She closed her brown eyes but remembered them and saw herself seeing Todd's body on her sheets, his smooth penis encircled by a pink ribbon she'd tied there. Happy Birthday to us all, they'd said earlier at the party. We're all twenty-six.

Marvin Waters was thirty-three and owns us all, they'd laughed. Old Marvin, the old sport. Himself thin and muscular—that exciting combination. And opening her eyes, going to lie down for a moment, her face covered with herbs in some fantastic decoction of mint and chervil and gelatin from sheep's feet and glacier water, she saw Marvin's penis too. Thicker like the pony's she'd once seen. That before nine and therefore with her handsome but pale father before he failed to float to safety in Laos.

There was Madelaine Woo at the office. Such power in the moon face. Like some brown full platter. All cheeks and such hair. Brilliant and coarse as the pony's.

She left the mirror and now she lay still in her warming bedroom. It is almost dark, she said to herself, and looked outside at the sugar-fine snow on branches.

She would not read anything on her bedside table; she didn't turn to the magazines or poems from newspapers her mother clipped and mailed. They were alike, so why think about her now? There's her picture, too, beyond my bare but hosed feet. Nice toes, he'd said. On a bus trip once, his fingers beginning there. You two are like twins, people said. And they were. Olive. Browns in eyes and hair. Once they'd changed roles at home for a whole weekend. Like that movie *Freaky Friday*, except there were no misadventures. She liked that word from one of her magazines. For her there never were. She knew she was only a bit too tall at five eleven. And a half, okay? A half. Not at all fat. Not thin, though. Not the anorexia of those hideous models.

We are just right, aren't we, she told the photographs as she flexed her toes.

And she turned on the bed when Ms. Bojangles leapt to the window ledge, meowed through the double glass. "Not now," she said. I'm going to rest. And yet once turned on her side away from the darkening day, she smiled. Comfortable in her clothes, the skin perfect now from mare's butter and summer savory. Smiled because we're alike, Ms. Bojangles and me here in my warming room. Not curious, that's all silliness. But active, energetic. But now after work, she decided not to drive this Friday night to exercise, and not to feed the cat now or herself, though on the edge of sleep that flowed like an exotic liquor Todd offered or like semen or some full-page ad all colors and promise, she remembered her duties and answered them like she always had—who had taught her that?—with miles to go before I sleep and miles to go before I sleep. Then, his house is in the village though.

Now there was a knock far away and she turned on her back and tried to listen for her own snore. That's what he'd joked. Like a bunkhouse. And she'd remembered movies. Old and distasteful men. Her grandparents dead long ago in a car wreck. She'd never seen them in photographs; oh, perhaps. But they were in their twenties and wearing fantastic clothes.

At the side door she said "Yes?" to the head made level with her waist by the three cement steps down to the carport. She pulled the thick robe around her, felt the chill on her ankles and up her calves.

"Hello, Nancy. Sorry . . . ," he said, and as he turned his face up into the light weakened by the filter of the screen door, she saw it was his unfamiliar face. The skin rough, raw on his left cheek, the one now turned north. The dark spots heightened by the cold. They looked at his hand on the doorknob. His other one at his collar, closing the material over white hairs like the snow-dusted grass near his feet. A large crumpled shopping bag sat on the bottom step.

"Sorry to bother you. I've left something in the shed. It's okay, I have a key." He dug in his pocket and lifted it. Shook it as if they were both deaf. Or children. Though she, nodding, saw he wasn't. Go away, she thought. And nodded vigorously, the updraft all over her now and robbing her of a lot of work on knees and buttocks.

Someday she would buy her own house, she thinks, and closes him out. I am a realtor after all. They turn back-to-back and she won't bother to watch him walk down the hill to the shed. Because she doesn't now consider him at all. Mr. Warrant. Her landlord; this house's owner. And later, eating something ultralight and microwaved though she always agrees, one, she doesn't have to watch her weight and, two, they really don't do food justice, she despises him and this rented house. Todd says live in the country. There he has a house and two ferocious fighting cocks. Why not uptown? Madelaine Woo asks. Forget a car and parking hassles. But this was truly one of the best deals in the city. And though it was a small house, the location wasn't so bad. She had moved here four years ago from college and only occasionally considered moving.

Later, the TV off, all the house gone from toasty to chilly, the red eye of the electric blanket reflected off mother's faces, father's face, everyone at the office in exotic costumes as bears and pigs all in great fun. The day someone said you can get your pussy tightened on group insurance and they'd laughed though she'd wondered if it were all a joke. She awoke and considered Mr. Warrant. And got up and out of bed and walked past the snoring Ms. Bojangles.

Wrapped in bathrobe and leg warmers and mittens, she hurried across the frozen yard and fumbled the shed door unlocked. She had never been curious. In school she was polite and attentive and knew, though such things weren't important really, she only loved activities that brought her to the attention of people—a few, a hundred at pep rallies. I was always beautiful, she knew, taking the flashlight from her robe pocket. And that was only eight years ago, less than eight really. Her fuller hips and breasts filled the robe now as she didn't wonder, wasn't curious about her curiosity about Mr. Warrant. Though there in bed in the chill far warmer than this dark shed, she remembered that he hadn't lived here in years and years. Before she had rented there had been the Squires, then someone else. He'd told her once—and now she surprised herself by recalling it—how he only had this and one other rental house. What had he done for a living? she thought, hurrying the beam over her scant holdings—yard tools she had bought once and now let the black boy use in the spring and summer.

But what would he have left and now needed? She stepped gingerly over rakes and cakes of mud, the smell all frigid oil and metal. Old, she thought, disgusted with greasy red shop towels and the yellowed refuse of newspapers someone had used for moving plates and vases. Maybe me, she thought. On a shelf at the back, the wind on her face through a knothole worrying her—she felt it on her drying lips; she envisioned spreading cracks, the deep furrows at too early an age—there was a box opened and empty. The gray duct tape having taken off layers of cardboard with it.

In the bathroom later, she looked at her face and decided on an emollient. And in bed she was as sure as she could be, having paid little attention to all that "out there," as she referred to it when the cute little black boy showed up biweekly, the box was his and had once been sealed tightly. She felt very tired. I've taxed my brain tonight, she said. She wished for someone. She moved in bed feeling, seeing, their two bodies all muscle and motion. His tanned skin on hers. The long shiny tube slowly inside. All oil and cream, sex the smell of spermicide, redolent of hospital corridors.

A week later there had been more snow and it had fallen wet and thick. Then there was a northern blast. From the top of the world, they'd said on TV. She liked that phrase. And there was a new man at the office. He was young and lonely. His hair lay on his neck in gorgeous tight curls. She talked to him and so did the others. Madelaine Woo almost swallowed him whole once at lunch.

But now with the thought of him, his body all beribboned in her mind, she took the River Road ramp and the Mill City Road instead of going her usual way from near the stadium to the office. "Nancy . . . ?" she said out loud and turned off the Cocteau Twins, the sound of it tiresome to her for the first time. She'd have to move on to another group.

Surely he's home, she said as she used her knowledge of the city, though there were never houses they handled over here past the cement plants. And, of course, heavy industries weren't their concern at all. As she glided past chained gates, she wondered how one sold those monsters. Old, blackened, rambling. No good lines, nothing clear and distinct. She imagined all the equipment inside and came away with only the vaguest outlines. Towering, greasy. She thought of the shed the other night and said the address where she mailed the rent checks. No ring to it. 718 Gilchrist Road. Mr. William Warrant. William. Bill. Billy. And she laughed and slowed to cross some train tracks.

There was nowhere to start really. He stood at the door, she, below, on the walk. She knew what he saw, his eyes all over her, his voice worried, disturbed. "Is there anything wrong at the house?" he asked. "No, nothing." And may I come in and yes, of course.

She had little time to focus; they walked through darkened rooms: furniture heavy, covered with chenille bedspreads, their tiny tassels and balls touching a monochrome, thick shag. Oh Jesus, she considered trying to sell all this. Saw it as a buyer she had ushered inside would, though in that case, she would have known everything already. She always did her homework, that's what they all said.

His eyes were a milky blue. From disease? she wondered, pausing before putting the cup of strong coffee to her lips. This afternoon the liver spots against the pale skin like ink on parchment.

"What was in the box?" she asked. You are so honestly straightforward, they'd always said. Yes, that's me, she answered. She saw herself, felt her neck arch. Looked down her nose so theatrically, they laughed.

He poured more coffee. From somewhere in cabinets he handed down a package of cake donuts all powdery like cocaine. That she avoided. And now these offerings all dry and, she knew, long past the freshness date she attempted to locate.

"Why?" he asked. She shrugged. And he took it up all naturally. There were no looks, tones in his voice. No reluctance.

No fear of the unknown. These she had painstakingly learned to recognize in buyers. Clients. People she served. My, you are good at this, the middle-aged men would say. And she knew that without these wives they would have said so young and attractive.

But not this old. Face sunk. Hands rough. He had been a foreman in one of those mills, she remembered, proud of her memory.

He told her about his wife. And how last week, "out of the blue," he said, he'd remembered the collection of mugs. See, look, and rising slowly, he brought them down from somewhere in the vast cabinets made of pressed wood. She saw their weak magnet locks. They clicked shut, the sound of Ms. Bojangles's claws on linoleum. And before her he spread out an array of heavy graceless mugs from all fifty states. Where we traveled together, you know. Oh, not all fifty, of course. We cheated a little. His laugh raspy and short. "I'd forgotten them, left them." And she'd loved them, too. And Nancy turned her listening away from the tone his voice took. It was outside her recognition. She nodded; she thought of them both living in this house. But she shook it out. A person simply can't picture most things. I'm all energy and light, she knew. No one ever said full of imagination. What good would that be? she asked herself. Know your strengths, everyone'd said.

But she listened some and drank too much bad coffee. Folger's, already ground. She tried thinking of it as espresso. Now that helped, made it better.

She had died ten years ago. Almost to the day last week. January 17. A Thursday. Almost to the day. "Ain't it something, Nancy?" He spoke her name and she was startled from her half reverie. Yes, you thought of the cups then. Lovely, she said, and touched the one from Texas, an oil derrick spouting oil.

From some deep back room he brought the picture of her at fifty. And there she was in her soft hands. Old, turning plump. The cheeks heavily powdered. The hair cropped close to her head. She remembered an awful, masculine picture of Gertrude Stein in some college textbook. All face and dikey. Women filling women's pussies.

But he talked on; she listened. She concentrated some. She focused herself. She decided, for some reason she wasn't at all curious about, to pay attention. And he told this and that. Someone dead in Korea. Illness. Travel. His wife did this, he said that.

All until it was dark early. You know how darkness comes on in January in the northeast. And she was too quickly ready to leave. Or not quick enough. Perhaps he was tired out, at the end, considering why all this had happened. Felt violated or foolish. She almost fled; he almost pushed her out and down the steps. They were terribly embarrassed. Full of civility and politeness of words and gestures. Agreed on the lateness, the cold, the need to drive carefully and quickly past the barren mills.

"Well, well," she said. You are quite a surprising girl. Ms. Bojangles would be speechless. She'd tell Madelaine Woo. No, she'd tell the new man at lunch in the art gallery cafeteria on Friday before the De Chirico exhibit and, she hoped, just hours before she tied lovely ribbons around his penis.

But you know that's not what happened at all. And no one in the world would have guessed it. Except her father, the only person who intuited things about her, who had skimmed along just above the jungle canopy with the smell of electrical fire in his nostrils, his face averted from flashing lights, the lightness of descent lessened only by the dead man behind him. At that moment, before the sea-green trees proved unlike waves, as hard as jade, he remembered her eight-year-old back ramrod straight at the piano stool, angry but unrelenting, demanding the keys obey her. And only he knew about her, understood everything that would take place without him. It'll end bad, he said to himself. But at that moment in October of 1969, it is impossible to know his exact reference.

So in two days she was back at Mr. Warrant's. It was Monday afternoon; there had been more snow, a deeper, bone-level cold. She knocked, using her left hand, the other arm full of groceries. As she shopped she had said, he'll like this and maybe this. And soon she'd collected eighty dollars' worth of exotics: pickled quails' eggs, a rare Tuscan cheese, the greenest, most expensive olive oil in the city.

But there was little surprise on Mr. Warrant's face. He led her to the kitchen. She chatted about the terrible weather. He told about his bad knee. "Here, right here," he said, and raised his pants leg. Without reservations. His shin discolored and hairless. As shiny as if he'd hot-waxed it. She looked away. Instead she cut onions into the olive oil, the expensive oil perfuming this room where they stood together. Until he sat and bent over a stack of crossword puzzle books.

Later he turned his nose up at the plate, complained about the small portions though he ate almost nothing at all. There was exotic salad, exotic pasta. She promised she'd bring over her new pasta machine. Then, at the table, at that second, her face toward his which looked away, his eyes on the crossword puzzle book on the table, at his elbow, she saw a lover she'd forgotten who'd run dough through a machine as he stood naked in the kitchen.

It's like he expects all this, she thought, eating demurely, pretending she was in a restaurant with music and candles and aquariums built into the walls. Here, really, it was too warm and awfully humid as if their bodies, the cooling oil, pasta, salad, puzzle books gave off water, sweated into the air. She watched droplets stream down the door behind him that opened onto some room or yard she'd never seen, that she didn't want to see. There at the table she promised she'd never learn about a yard or room or garage or if there was a car or anything else at all.

She took an interest in Mr. Warrant's puzzles. In some other room removed from the kitchen, where there were no odors of expensive oils and seasonings, they sat at a card table in the middle of furniture covered with chenille bedspreads. Onstage like chess champions, she thought. But a ghost audience.

"You're a smart one," he said. "Yep, you are a smart one." And she was surprised at his limited vocabulary. Vocabulary, she said to herself, and realized it was a word from school, further surprised she could fill out the puzzles with ease. But they're easy, of course. While he suffered over them. "No, don't tell me now. Keep quiet." His voice a command. Like Todd in throaty, aroused tones, telling her to roll onto her stomach.

She smelled him, imbibed him. What is this but age? And she couldn't place any of it exactly. Not among the most narrowly focused recollections. Not leather she'd smelled in France. Or fabrics in shops. Or the smell of any man anywhere before. Wasn't it a house whose door she had just unlocked? On a tree-lined street, broken sidewalk a disadvantage. She saw clients stepping over it dramatically, arching eyebrows. A house on the edge somewhere in Pittsfield maybe. Almost a dozen things. Fashionable, ghetto, expensive, cheap. But the air when she opens it first, alone, doing her homework. God, she's devoted, hard-driving, a hell-of-an-agent. Agent, she liked the word. A secret agent. Words and puzzles; she breathed in again. She's not wearing underwear, you know. The young office boys talked at the cooler under the aerial view of the city they sold off piece by piece. She bends over for fun. To tease. But no, she never teased. Or not really.

The odor of this very old man. Only a little like walls in houses that almost sell but never do. They talk about nothing at all. She cleans up but leaves her watch on the window ledge as the excuse for coming back she doesn't need. He sleeps at the card table a deep, dead sleep. There is no snoring, no movement. He is dead, she thinks, and cannot touch him; not the weak-muscled arm, even the shoulder under the thin shirt. She goes out and home and takes a long, hot shower, smells her skin, and ladles it with balm of peaches and placenta.

But every night she is there, at the door. Mr. Warrant's face expressionless. I am a social worker, she thinks. That's what it's like to him.

She moves about the house. It is unsalable. It is huge and amorphous, shifting and dark with those high, narrow windows people sold and bought once which look out into treetops and sky sliced by power lines. Add to that the weakness of his small-wattage bulbs. But no, she says, I'll make do with it all like this. Exactly. Though from room to room she is lost. And turning back around, finds the door to the kitchen or the room with him at the card table. As if there were fifteen kitchens and rooms with card tables. All off a room dreadfully dark, the furniture towering. Like her images of the barren mills. His house a closed factory, without production. Waiting for nothing at all. The odor of the shed, of its newspapers and grease, confined her for a time to the two rooms where every night they worked their way through endless puzzles. "You are bright." I am also beautiful with perfect hips, she told herself. Not many can say that—perfect hips. Absolutely perfect. Sculpture, one had said. Brown. Delicious. Some foreign fruit. A soufflé. Risen to perfection.

Often he dozed profoundly. She straightened the kitchen, put her graceful fingers into deep and obscure cabinets. The cups, those mugs, the plates dulled by a century of bacon grease.

They watched TV, "Wheel of Fortune." He called her Joyce. "Who?" she'd turned to ask over the card table scattered with puzzle books. "What?" he answered her. "Joyce 'who'?" His eyes snapped back to the expensive gifts for the winning contestant. As exotic and foreign to him as sapphires and camels—an animal she'd ridden with pleasure in Cairo; a gem she'd been given more than once.

She read her magazines, her magnificent suit attracting the chenille to it, mixing with Ms. Bojangles's yellow hair. Even you could never sell this house, she told herself. What did I just say? Joyce, who?

Then she stayed the night. She planned nothing. Why? What

do you plan? Planning was for work. She had slept with Marvin again. He had eaten strawberry jam off her clitoris. She had screamed for the first time some sound that had sent Ms. Bojangles tearing down the hall to sit near the heat vent and had jerked Marvin's head up. In the dark his eyes like Negroes' in old movies. Feets do yo stuff. "Nancy, my god, did I hurt you?" But she lay perfectly still, speechless. At first it was because she had no reason to give him, then it was a game, finally she couldn't bear to talk. He dressed and drove away, the rumble of his Lancia like thunder through frozen February air at three in the morning.

They had eaten bacon sandwiches and played the puzzles. She was getting worse; he was improving. They watched "Wheel of Fortune" and, after scouring the ancient black iron skillet, she shook him gently, averting her eyes from the thick strand of saliva connecting the corner of his lip to a liver spot on the back of his hand the shape of Chile. Let's go there, the German lover had pointed at a poster in a window. Santiago de Chile. The street full of assured brown faces.

She led him through the darkness from the card table to the bedroom she had guessed at but never been in. And inside it was the same dark towering furniture, a room from Dickens, she thought, surprising herself with an image of some woodcut from a high school library book.

She undressed in a frenzy, upsetting herself a little. This isn't like me at all. Hurrying is spoiling it, she thought. But she turned off the light, left her clothes in a pile, and slid between the covers. The sheets were clammy, they felt as if they'd never warm. She rolled side to side and finally lay still, turned her eyes to Mr. Warrant, who sat heavily on the opposite edge of the bed. Slowly he took off his slippers. Still sitting, he removed his pants. And in the twilight from some outside light through the half-opened blinds, she shuddered. The more he took off—old-fashioned undershirt like Madelaine Woo wore to picnics, her nipples huge rosettes, the billowing boxer shorts—the smaller he became until lying next to her, letting out a heavy sigh, he was nothing at all. She was the weight in the bed. And when she turned toward him, he rolled to meet her. And the instant they touched his whole body twitched as if he'd been electrified like those TV patients with paddles to their chests.

"Nancy!" he said. "What is this? My God, girl. My heavens. This isn't . . ." But he didn't finish. And neither could she, though, her hands on his thin leg, her mind snagged the sentence and tried to complete it. This isn't. But positive as always—as they always said, she took the lemons of life and made lemonade—she ran her freshly oiled fingers up his thigh.

Her graceful fingers found his penis and massaged it carefully. She located its thick undervein and followed it with long reassuring strokes. But there was no length to it. His scrotum was a thick still bag in her palm. And when she ducked her head under the covers, her tongue ready to moisten, coax, he held her head still. In the absolute dark her nose touched his hairless chest and she breathed in all the unusual odors. She felt his chest heave in spasms and she listened to him cry through the heavy damp quilts. For a long time she rested, his hand having released her hair, and she heard his stomach rumble from the bacon. She smelled his age like all old things that weren't people. Her own grandparents had died young. She had never sold a nursing home. Old people never came up to her on the streets. Distant grandchildren always put their useless houses on the market.

She came up from the covers into the twilight and listened to Mr. Warrant, on the edge of deep sleep, on the precipice of years of dreams that combined and recombined, mumble about Joyce and his wife and someone else, Bob or Rob, or maybe not that name at all. The tides at Inchon. Her own name, Nancy, called out once as if it were punctuation, an exclamation point. Or was it a question mark? Nancy? This isn't . . .

She lay stretched out next to him and didn't strain to listen, to decipher his weightless words as airy as his body next to hers. She was substantial, lotioned, perfumed, ready for anything. But slowly she saw herself right in this room lighted by the streetlight she passed every afternoon now when she drove straight here from work. "Hey, I've been phoning you," Marvin said. The newest man, too. Your machine broken? Yes, it is, she said. And brought Ms. Bojangles and put her out of sight in a far room where they were both sure of mice, the chenille balls offering unlimited entertainment.

Then she was eager for it all to be done with—the dinners with little variation between fried foods; endless puzzles; television—so in the twilight she could listen to his weightless digressions and fill herself with his odor, the pungency of the room, the licorice smell of all the photographs, the gray underwear. The carpet full of pieces of paper; underneath the bed, the exposed springs a jungle of cobwebs and lint. There must be remnants of her in there, Nancy said to herself. For now, in the afternoons, before fried pork chops, strips of mealy steak, she would come in here and raise the blinds, her one act of alteration, and examine drawers and closets.

But there was nothing left of hers except a closet of empty hangers wrapped in yarn, cloth flowers entwining the crooks. And empty bureau drawers; his dingy clothes all in one shallow top drawer. Under pajamas never out of their wrappers, she found a pistol but jerked away from it. The chill on its handle like the cold of all inanimate metal. She recalled the shed, the gloom of all the closed factories lining her route here.

She drank in everything, you know. Her father wouldn't have been a bit surprised; her mother, always out of mind, would have been properly scandalized. Her fellow workers remarked on her calm. Someone thought she was pregnant; impossible given the impossibility of such from the small soft penis she only cupped as he told her about the drowned boy at Inchon; the brother who'd stolen his girl when they were teenagers and who lived for thirty years in a VA hospital because he lay down on the outskirts of Metz and refused to advance or retreat, to take any further actions against the enemy.

Madelaine Woo said, "You look tired," and they both saw her face left unpampered. The emollients, placentas, balms of tarragon, and avocadoes at home in the empty house.

She took herself a history. She forgot Ms. Bojangles in the far room living off mice and quickly forgetting about people. The boy at Inchon became her lover. The penis in her hand swelled in her mind and took her so huge it filled her anus too. Sometimes she moaned as Mr. Warrant talked. At puzzletime she brought out yellowed ones she had found and carefully erased. So that the answers were references to men and events thirty years ago. Mr. Warrant was surprised because he thought everyone had forgotten. "My God," he'd say. "Nancy, look at this. Nancy, see here?"

She moved more slowly. Sensuous; she's practicing for something, someone, they'd said at the office. She dropped out of fashion but they all opened their mouths in excitement. She is beautiful, they all agreed. She is magnificent. Her hips are perfect. A delicious soufflé.

In the mirror she examined her face. She scrubbed away the makeup. She had passed a point somewhere recently, she knew. Once, without it, she was a child, a featureless girl. But now she was almost eyebrowless and a painful plain. I'm this way now. Belonging to this mirror and this unsalable place. I do my work, but I move more slowly. I think, but often I am there waiting for twilight and the absence of his body. I have always had the passion of pursuit, so I'll pursue this. All of this. This isn't . . . she remembered. But now nodded at these eyes in the mirror and said "Yes, it is" out loud.

She discovered the cat and called it Ms. Bojangles again. She abandoned the plates high in the dark towering cabinets to all the upwafting grease. She cut her hair too short. They were surprised. Her father slammed into the treetops in 1969 and wished her luck, never thought of his wife, cried out a moment before dissolution at his daughter's terrible purposefulness which could always give pain.

And here's the contrast: As limbs whipped the metal to shreds, he only wanted to live. And live everything again at once—to be her age, younger, older, older than anyone he'd ever met. Be an ancient man protected from harm on a screened porch. The very last thought the amorphous face, constantly changing in some movie he'd seen once.

But not Nancy, not now. Now she came to Mr. Warrant's and fried foods, worked puzzles, watched TV, lay next to his minute body, her own body more weightless from not soaking in herbed butters and comfit of womb of lamb.

What is she doing? they began to wonder. Did you notice too? And Madelaine Woo nodded her flat moon face like the affirmation of an Asian goddess. Her clothes aren't straightened. And no one but the two "gopher" boys talked about her odor. The smell of sour milk or of meat grease poorly doused with Chanel.

Marvin believed it might be drugs but didn't say that to anyone; instead he turned his attention to someone in the accounting department. Only Madelaine asked and, receiving a vacant stare, didn't ask again for over two months until she cajoled Nancy to lunch at a new restaurant full of aquariums and gorgeous waiters in tight Italian pants that zipped up the side.

"What is wrong? What's happened? Are you ill? You had a mammogram last month . . . is that it? Nancy, can I help? Everyone's worried sick about you."

And on and on until she had stopped, her face flushed, her eyes full of tears. Real tears for me, Nancy thought, and patted Madelaine's hand and told her everything would be fine soon. Only a temporary personal problem. "It's my mother . . . she's terribly sick," she told her. And added the threat of cancer since Madelaine had mentioned the mammogram.

And later in one of the rooms, her rumpled suit collecting cat hair, chenille threads, the odor of pork sausage and eggs for supper, she was sorry for lying, for sacrificing her mother, and wondered what if it were true.

But she breathed in the age, was, to her mind, older than her mother, than the man she slept next to every night. Once he had reached for her, his small hand running up her thigh. But she had brushed him away and felt sincere and elevated by her dismissal. "Maybe tomorrow night," she whispered into his deaf ear. "Huh?" "Not now, later," she spoke up, her voice muffled by carpet, drapes, afghans.

She still did well at selling houses. She's lost almost all of her beauty, the newer man said. The newest woman had never seen it. "But not her touch; no, she's still got that magic touch."

I'm learning everything, she thought. About it all. And she took on the older clients, men who wanted to rub up against her in narrow doorways in empty office buildings. Their wives in other cities. And she stayed still for them, her eyes averted, until they both passed into long corridors scuffed by mailing carts.

By now she had practically emptied her house. There were a few clothes, all the photographs, the answering machine all lighted up, the tape crammed with voices and whining beeps.

She never altered a single thing at Mr. Warrant's. She tucked her underwear in the drawer below his, she drank disgustingly thick whole milk. She delighted in the filtered light through the blinds. She roared her car past the destroyed mills; it rocketed over the uneven tracks.

Until a Saturday morning when she brought the heavy pistol from the drawer and sat on the bed. Their bed, she said to herself. It was like a movie pistol, the barrel long and octagonal. She counted its sides more than once.

She recollected a photograph whose absence or perhaps presence somewhere else—at her mother's, not in albums but in shoeless boxes?—worried her. It wasn't her father but a friend of his in uniform wearing a pistol in a waxy brown scabbard.

"A fellow officer," she heard him say. His voice was a young man's voice in her ears.

She believed it was unloaded, thought she'd seen the cartridges in a drawer or in a jar in some other room. But she couldn't be sure and so quickly brought the barrel up to her lips and opened wide. "Ouch, your teeth!" the German had shouted. And a joke, long ago though only in high school, wasn't it? About the desire for fold-back teeth in a woman. This thickness on her tongue and mouth like lava, or an animal burrowing in the throat.

She sucked the metal of it. All greasy and shedlike. Garages and body shops. The litter of unsalable things.

But you know she didn't bleed until almost sixty hours later. It was a little before two in the morning when she sat up and said "Oh Jesus" because she had never done something like this.

"What's wrong? Nancy?" And his back's joints popping, Mr. Warrant sat up. "Goddammit," he shouted and pulled away from her.

They fumbled in the dark, their legs sticky from her blood until he thumbed on the light, its three-way bulb only working on low, barely illuminating the two of them there, the covers flung back and Nancy's panties the chocolate red of refused blood.

"Christ, I'm sorry," she said, and stood and surveyed the damage, her mind full of the necessity for towels, sheets, had it gone through to the mattress? Thinking, there really is no other bed.

"Good God," Mr. Warrant said looking up at her, past stained clothes, his eyes wide.

She came around to him and sat, taking his shoulders, forcing his face away. He thought it was his blood, she said to herself. "It's all right . . . it's okay . . . it's mine. I'll go get some towels and clean sheets."

"No, no," he mumbled, his lips still thick from sleep. Both their breaths the concoction of the days' odors.

"I didn't remember the blood, you know."

Nancy nudged him out to arm's length. His wispy hair like a baby's, his face discolored on one side. "It's been thirty years I guess. All that . . . all of that." She watched him look at her differently. She believed he wanted to grab the covers up or flee. His face was full of fear, and she knew hers was too. She believed they sat there looking exactly the same. She clenched his shoulders, her fingers dug into his flimsy flesh.

Nancy worked quickly for almost half an hour until she finished and they slept. She had refused to leave. She wouldn't dare go to the convenience store near the loop, out past the foundries. Instead she had folded one of his undershirts into a roll and pulled it between her legs.

"She's changed," the newer man said. But they never knew what they meant by that. And once, overhearing Marvin talk about the new girl he'd slept with, she had stepped around the corner just to shut him up for a moment. The triumph, she knew, only lasted until she was out of earshot.

She went back once a week for over a month, but the doors were locked, and she never knocked, and though she had keys, she never put them into any of the locks.

Her clothes came in boxes left in her carport or on the tiny front porch. They came over a period of weeks. One she recognized as the carton that had held the mugs. Later, she'd gone out to the shed and unlocked it and saw he had taken all the boxes.

She handled some houses better now. She found she was less afraid when she saw buckled sidewalks and walls patterned by the bright squares from removed pictures and photographs.

"You scared me," he had printed on the lid of one of the first boxes with a felt-tipped marker. She pictured his hand working a puzzle.

Two months later she phoned him and his voice was as she remembered it, but now she knew he had never talked to her much and had never, she believed, looked her in the eyes until the night she had bled on them both.

"Hello, Mr. Warrant," and she was pleased his voice was firm and not surprised. Neither hung up because of any of a dozen unarticulated thoughts that rushed like cold air, then hot, through both their minds. But though she begged him, he refused to take any rent at all and, until she moved downtown with Ms. Bojangles and across the courtyard from Madelaine Woo, he returned every month's check in a brown envelope with the return address of some company carefully marked through.

RESIDUE

Chris had come to this Asian desert for no good reasons. Sure, he'd gotten nervous the first month after the army'd finished with him. And, February, over a year ago, he'd met her dancing at some club across the county line where liquor stores stayed open to midnight and pitchers of beer in the honky-tonks were twice as expensive as they should have been.

But then he ran away from her. That's what he called it himself. *I've run away.* And once he'd done that, once he'd piled his things under the pickup's leaking camper top, he didn't stop in Childress or Flatonia or even in Houston where he planned to stop—where so many others had stopped over the last hundred years of running that direction from all the other directions.

Once out the door—her face on the pillow wiped clean of makeup, eyebrowless, twenty years older than lounge light and bedside lamps revealed; open and slack—he was fantastically weightless. Like a balloon let loose, he jettisoned his air, voided the ballast of her, then his pickup, finally even his split and wired suitcase full of cassette tapes and cigarettes. Until he floated gently to earth here in this high Asian desert. To this town with no pronounceable name. Goatville, they called it. First the survey party chief, Walliston, had said that over a gritty, almost flat St. Pauli's Girl. Then he and the other instrument man, Paddy, had repeated it. Then they'd all said it to themselves in their small rooms as the cool spring had given way to an awful summer heat which only intensified the bone-numbing nights. All the day's repressive heat sucked cleanly away within an hour of sundown. The chilled metal frames of their beds betraying the passionless ritual of masturbation. Or their semen saved up for a couple of days to splatter the neck and nipples; sperm and breath the only warmth in the bare rooms. Watch faces flashing in the light of desert stars.

Somewhere to the east, on this vast plain as flat as the military haircut he'd kept, Dutchmen were planning a dam across a river gorge. He'd seen the river from the airplane and later crossed it in a Jeep, the water a jade-and-red slug stretched out in the sand. But in Goatville the river was several hard hours away, looping in a gradual decline to the south and west.

So the three of them took out level loops. They carried numbers from the top of a seven-foot cement post sunk in the red sand. The two hired rodmen were locals. Taught to rest the numbered rod on the brass cap and to rock it gently back and forth. Quite natural to these two who spoke fragmented English and rocked in their prayers at noon, a lighted candle stuck to the truck bumper, a prayer wheel in each hand. Chants and moans. Some local religion born of immense distances, landscapes of red and ocher, skies painfully blue and clear. The name of god sent flying on the wind that guttered the candle and spun the wheel.

They took numbers out into the desert. They began at the brass cap, blinding in the sun. The butt of the rod kissing metal to metal. Each day the loops grew longer, farther from the cement post. An oval in the field book becoming an oval of numbers. The desert's topography betraying itself to the tenth of a foot. 4.7. 5.2.

One day Chris realized how unbelievably flat it was, and he wondered how long ago the others had come to the same conclusion; he knew he was the last. He stared through the Gurley level. They were weightless by now. The liquids and salts that held them down all gone, replaced by special brews and tablets. Walliston sitting in the open door of the Suburban, its huge balloon tires lifting him three feet off the ground.

Turning back, his eyeball was again sucked into the light and wavering heat of the tube. He'd spat out thousands of numbers in three months even with a week in the nearest city seven hundred miles away to the south and west. There had been St. Pauli's Girl there, too. And noise and the thick Eurasian woman who took you in her mouth and pulled your balls down to your knees until pain forced a shriek. The shriek eaten by her and all the crash of buses and mopeds outside in the yellow hazy air.

Paddy lay up under the truck, his eyes safely behind a forearm. His last two-hour stint at reading the rod done. So, finally, Walliston would step down and slowly wave his arms, the watch crystal catching the declining brilliance in a threat of tomorrow's slow climb and fall.

In the distance Chan #1 shouldered the rod they seldom had to telescope past its first section. Most of the numbers falling between 4.2 and 5.0. The dry streambeds packed with sand.

He watched Chan #2 clap and dance around his brother rodman. Their loose brown-and-white clothes whipping in some wind not found here a hundred yards to their west.

Sometimes he wanted all the things he'd never liked. There could be snow covering this landscape of sere waist-high brush and scattered piles of dull stone. Where's the party, chief? they'd kidded earlier. That and all the other old surveying jokes. But they no longer enthusiastically completed field books at night in the bare front room of the hotel. And now no one dropped by to look at them; the first foreigners in over four years. The last man an Argentinean who'd arrived in a flurry of language and left again immediately. No one sure of what he'd wanted though they'd all come running to offer suggested routes, times of day to depart, evaluations of tire treads and jerrycans.

Once they'd figured that six more months would see them through. But there were the delays of equipment repair, gasoline replenishment, sandstorms rising out of the west like mile-high red surf. The light gone, not filtered away but absent. The vast red wave cascading down, filling everything. Ears and nostrils. Unopened beer cans and toothpaste tubes. Carburetors. The fine screw adjustments of instruments.

Deutschmarks filled their accounts in the distant city. New clothes came one day and they hurried inside to change and laugh. The three of them played cards with the faded deck, the plastic backing sanded away already. The two Chans laughing and talking at them in their broken Empire English. Pointing and shaking their heads as cigarettes changed piles. Paddy's Salems producing a groan from the other two who scooped them in begrudgingly.

Making use of the long light of summer, they worked six days a week. From six until noon; four until eight. On what they estimated was Sunday, they stayed in the hotel near the one well in the middle of town. Town from their windows on the second floor consisting of two perpendicular streets.

From his window Chris saw mud roofs, a foolish tethered goat that bled from its bound leg. Stupid to struggle, he thought. He smelled sand and heat. At the town's edge the afternoon sun destroyed everything beyond with fantastic undulations. He rubbed his eyes.

They forgot things. Couldn't recall old addresses, the tight curl of pubic hair, the whorls lost in the buzz of a thousand prayer wheels spinning atop courtyard walls. Endless prayers, he thought, ironically generated by the gods for the gods. A wonderful joke by the people living in solitude on such an endless, arid plain.

This desert did what he soon hoped it might with the same anxious expectations you have in a doctor's waiting room. Is this the time or not? And, finally, just come on, just come out with it. He shaved before dinner. They ate without the Chans on these supposed Sundays and only the plump owner and his plumper wife broke the silence, laying mismatched silverware and enigmatic platters with the double lightning flashes of the SS crowding their borders.

There was simple reduction. No trees. Some water. Few birds. The scurry of lizards inside and out. Their own voices low out there by the Suburban in the late afternoon as they folded the tripod, loaded the rod in its case. The Chans already in the truck turning the radio from hiss to hiss. Walliston was from Ohio. He had one old son who drank. Paddy was fifty-six and his teeth occupied all his attention. If Chris looked into Paddy's eyes they never really looked back but down a little at the perpetual curl on Paddy's lips. Tongue prying. Thumbnail picking.

There were these hardships but no dangers. The company's universally recognized logo on the truck obviated a lot. Camaraderie had flared and flickered. Walliston slept the unbelievable sleep of hard work well done. Paddy paced, felt his jaw, masturbated regularly into a sock that Chan #1's sister would wash later in the red water from the well next door.

Then the Suburban broke down, the transmission full of sand that had slipped past seals and evaded the lubrication of heavy oil. All in a little more than three months. So now Paddy took things apart, lost bolts off the blanket, scrambled out from underneath, and pounded his jaw, fists a blur.

But Chris only looked on. From their first meeting in the city to the southwest he had said he knew levels and transits and inhospitable places—though he'd lied because he'd been stationed in Louisiana and Kentucky—but not a goddamned thing else.

He watched Paddy kick the tires and scatter the ugly chickens and he thought about how easily the Deutschmarks accumulated. Level loops were the easiest thing. Not like construction or highway surveying. Anybody could learn in half a day. How to set up, level out, read the rod—hold it if you had to—and fill in the field book. Backsights, foresights, the whole theory of elevations.

They'd have to wait for the scheduled resupply in five days, and someone would go back on the dilapidated Chevy flatbed, the local irregular bus, into the larger Goatville to cable for a mechanic. "Fuck it," Paddy stuttered over aching teeth, grit on all their tongues, fur in their throats.

So Chris went back early and sat on the minuscule balcony and drank St. Pauli's Girl and thought and remembered and let the remainder of the day's heat suck it away. Take this year and that one too. Take her and him and leave me only residue, salt. Evaporation. Only movements are essential to remember in the desert. One has to be careful with the body. The mind is expected to wander in search of something to latch on to. That brush. The distant hills like memories of hills. All colors shades of red. His past wasn't very much at forty-four and so mandated a slow yield to avoid the heat and distances from just taking it all at once. He was regimented, the loss was scheduled. This space had absorbed a Roman legion, he'd read in a magazine he'd bought in the city after the Eurasian woman had caused him pain. At the old dam farther south it had never rained. It had never rained. What dimension vacuum do such facts create?

It gave looming mirages back. But they weighed nothing and were themselves taken from somewhere else and brought here by fractured light. *Fata morgana,* the Italians called them.

They had the usual goat stew and thick-skinned beans and sharp sour cheese. St. Pauli's too. After dinner he lay down in the faded blue room. He looked at the two posters he'd bought in the city. In one a naked woman was bent over, her face leering over a shoulder, her royal-blue fingernails pulling her shaved pussy apart. In the other a red Porsche sped down a winding coastal highway, the water far below almost transparent. Above the road there were pines and cedars. He rose from the bed and walked across to the posters. If you looked closely, you could almost make out the man driving behind the reflective sheen of the windshield. The woman had rows of pimples on her ass. He took the posters down and carefully folded them at the rough table. He hoped he would get to go cable for the mechanic so he could buy some new decorations.

But Walliston climbed on the smoking, rattling Chevy flatbed. Smiling and waving, he wedged in between cardboard boxes and a lame family going for medicine or prayer. And since they'd already cleaned and adjusted all the equipment over the last several days, he'd left them a series of level loops they'd saved for just such a time. Small ovals near the village, up to the northwest and down back to the brass cap; they could walk, toting the equipment. But Paddy suddenly produced a quart of Boodles at supper and poured it down like ice water. The next morning, which they supposed to be Wednesday, Paddy didn't answer the knocks on the sagging door. When Chris pushed it open, Paddy was asleep in a tangle of loosened clothes and split sheets. Two empty bottles in the middle of the floor.

Paddy's blind drunkenness was unexpected. St. Pauli's was one thing. How the hell had he managed to hide such a supply of hard liquor? He wondered if Paddy'd been drinking on the sly all along. Chris sat that day and the next morning in his room or in the front room downstairs. The two Chans staring in at the door, the strong light behind them. He wanted to rest here too. For a couple of days. Or for a week. Walliston would sputter and pace but that would pass quickly enough. The Deutschmarks flooded in whether he had his eye to the Gurley or down the throat of a beer bottle.

But on Friday he rose early, the chill of the night on his watch face and the useless keys to the Suburban. Without thinking, he sent Chan #1 home and kept the other, who babbled in patois and ran to the truck to jerk out everything until Chris said no, no, and swore and pushed the too-anxious fellow aside.

There were no mirages in the chill as the two walked the loop out from the tarnished cap. Backsight. Foresight. Break down the light metal tripod. Then level it out again. 4.6. 4.8. The level bubble shifting in the sand. His legs splayed away from the tripod. Chan #2 distorted in the first undulations of heat. He looked, waved, copied his own thoughts. Thoughts in numbers only. He believed that was why he had gotten up in the dark and dressed. The desert had almost sucked him clean by now. Besides the numbers and the blue room at night little remained except the expectations of scenery and images of Deutschmarks falling through blank space. He wondered again, at noon, as they lay behind a desiccated bush, where Paddy'd kept the gin until now. He shrugged and folded his paper lunch bag. The swig of red water still on his tongue.

"So, you married?"

He turned on his side away from Chan #2 and put his arm across his face. He shook his head. But the stocky Chan talked on, more than he ever had before though Walliston liked to rib them, make them say foolish things, and turn to Paddy and him and arch his eyebrows.

"Here, you see this?" There was the crinkle of unrolled paper and Chan #2 held over Chris's shoulder the poster Chris had pulled down a few days ago. The blue fingernails and shaved pussy a strange sight behind the low brown bush, its leaves almost completely withdrawn, minuscule and waxy.

"I found it, you see. Behind Xiang's, in rubbish." Chan #2 laughed and he heard him sit up. The sound of fine falling sand.

Chris turned onto his back, sat up on his elbows. "It's a picture, that's all it is. You can have it."

Chan #2 shook his grinning round face; his teeth were yellow stumps. He smelled of smoke and cheese. His face, his hands on the opened poster motionless. His deferential smile glowed.

To the west they watched a long row of date palms. Underneath them men and camels moved. There were tents billowing in the wind. The whole looming mirage three feet off the ground.

"You know about women I bet. Anyone can see you do. With such pictures."

"Sure, if you say so. But you can have that . . . here," and he sat up and took the woman and folded her carefully, leaving half her face, one terribly lewd eye staring, and put it on Chan #2's lap. He noticed Chan was missing the top of his left thumb above the knuckle. It ended in a loose tuck of skin that wiggled as he took the poster and looked down into the woman's face.

They worked on. The heat forcing several rests, spoiling a regular day's routine. But he said fuck them; fuck Walliston and Paddy. They worked their way back to the brass cap. He looked, read numbers. Recorded them. 4.4. 5.2. 4.9. His eye now seeing the maimed thumb on the side of the rod. The grinning face seen in silence through the heat devils rising up to dance with and tease distances.

They locked the cases in the Suburban. He walked up the street toward the hotel, but Chan #2 pulled at his sleeve. He turned and rubbed his aching eyes. His mind only on beer and the thick stew and sweetened, reconstituted dried fruit.

The broad face too close to him in actuality. "I please ask question?" Chan #2 closed his eyes for a moment. "Mr. Chris . . . if can?" His smile faltered.

Chris breathed in the town smells. Beyond the last mud brick house and across a tremendous distance he made out the mountains that surrounded the plain.

"What is it? What do you want?"

"You know about women; you married."

"No, I told you no."

"I like to ask question."

Two small boys herded emaciated sheep around them toward the water trough at the lip of the well. The wind picked up and sent the prayer wheels clattering.

"What is it?"

Chan #2 grinned and pulled him across to a low stone wall. Chris sat; the little man sat on his left hip, hunkered close, his head shoulder high.

"I do wrong, you think? What, then, I do? She say no, no, not now, it too late for that, but . . ." Chan stopped and looked at him, brought his head up, straightened his back. There was no trace of a grin now. He leaned back and began again, slowly, telling how his wife had been eight months pregnant with their first child and how he couldn't help himself after he'd had too much fun and drink at some sort of card game. He had come home near dawn and the sight of her huge tight belly had driven him wild. He'd pulled her to him. It was awkward, but he hadn't stopped.

Chris listened and then he stopped Chan #2 with a pat on his shoulder.

"But it the child, too, you see. Little girl already shamed she no boy. But born funny, arms cross chest," and Chan folded his own. "We massage with oil and say prayers, but them not unfold. Not once in a year."

"Those things happen." And he stood and looked down at Chan #2. It was twilight and windy and growing cool. Chris couldn't imagine any of the women he'd known with bellies full of anything but food and drink. Inside them there was pleasure and noise. They plunged together. Besides, she'd been too old and he'd never wanted anything but the path of least resistance. Exactly what this place offered. With everything cooked off, only the residue remains. And that, in time, would vanish. A path with no resistance.

Chan followed behind him to the hotel. They talked at the door about tomorrow and Chan smiled and nodded. But then he spoke low and quick. "She and baby go to parents, you see, Mr. Chris. What I say to her, you think? You know; such a man as you know."

He went inside. Paddy was at the table finishing his meal. He never said anything and barely looked up. Instead he exaggerated his actions. Poured the Boodles in high arcs into the coffee mug. The two of them ate goat stew off the Nazi insignias.

In his blue room he heard the wind against the closed balcony doors and he hoped for a storm that would fall over everything. Sand in gin and transmissions. He felt how the howl increased the cold and how the cold demanded thoughts and movements for warmth. He arched his body under the covers, his mind's eye in the Gurley seeing Chan's thumb. He crossed his hands over his chest. He put them down at his side. He wanted absolutely nothing for himself. He demanded it.

Early the next morning he sent Chan #2 home and had Chan #1 wakened. He took him first to the brass cap and then into the desert. But after ten, and at a distance of a hundred meters, the work didn't matter. This day proved the hottest of the summer and the intense heat fractured the air between them, twisting the distant rod and maiming numbers and hands. They packed up and turned back toward the village.

At noon he left Chan at the Suburban to square things away, but he took the Gurley to the hotel. At almost one o'clock in the morning, when the bright scimitar moon rose from behind the mountains, the level brought its razor edge down close to his eye. This was something he hadn't done in years. And the reaction now was the same as then, and he didn't know why this was. Come see this, he wanted to say. You should come see this.

Half the street below was in darkness; his only companion was the same tethered, restless goat.

HISTOIRE DE MON TEMPS

"Voiture," I say, listening to the whine of the pickup's mud tires on asphalt. Know it's on the ridge behind me, a mile away. I turn my back to the road. Imagine that my weak vision goes far beyond the four-strand barbed-wire fence to the cows I can smell pissing. To the newest calves I hear now in this new early March grass. Up to the hills covered with some oaks but mostly pines Mothermae called "evergreens."

"Voiture," I say when the sound changes. Passing over the bridge where the grate opens. I almost piss on myself, my hand cupped in my open overalls. I feel then smell a trickle. Mothermae pulling the chocolate skin back, the head a pink like here, these phlox at my feet. Flocks of sheep, I used to think. I almost turn to look at the coming truck. Voiture I picked up right here against this post. The one I watched them replace the year we spent most of the summer outside when they brought in the hay.

"Hey, look at this. Rudy, look at all this."

Mothermae and I listened to them from the dry creek that crosses the open fields, the biggest under a cloud of dust from their haying. She held onto my neck, our breaths struggling in both our throats.

"Voiture!" I try to yell, keeping my back to it as it screams past. Make my lips move. The scrap of paper over the stove, stuck to the wall with tacks or spit. English-French, French-English, the other, thicker paper says. "Voiture!" I scream as I face the empty road that goes uphill, crosses the bridge, and climbs to the straight green line of pines. "Evergreens."

"Hobo camp," Rudy had said. A big blond man catching the light. His bare chest yellowed even more by pieces of hay. I could see the flecks of dirt muddied at his neck. Mothermae's face turned away. I saw them through the broken window. They tossed it all out but left our scraps of paper on the walls. Then, later, a day and a night. The evergreen straw a nice bed up on the bank in the sapling thicket. The sky cloudless until late afternoon but no rain. They burned our gleaned mattress and chest of drawers, and the heat from the diesel cracked the mirror. I saw them in it, looking down, turning black, then its weak silvered back broke.

"Niggers, I'll bet," Rudy said. And the other man nodded before they unloaded hay again, stacking it to the ceiling; the old house groaning. They didn't seem to notice the garden, didn't say a word about the flowers. "We ought to bring the dozer over sometime," Rudy's friend said, "and level it. Put up a decent hay barn." But Rudy shrugged, the muscles shadowing on his back and that was then. That year.

Just a few years later they changed the Bridger Creek sign. The fall after Mothermae died they came and took it down—all full of .22 holes. I heard someone that bad winter and only at night shoot and shoot. Fifty or more times. She was sick always by then with the fever, the gas swelling her stomach like the dead on the highway. She'd let it go with a long, soft noise.

Before it had said Bridgett Creek. But the road crew didn't seem to mind. I watched all morning. They kept me from the grate I'd just found on up the hill on the other side. Now I walk carefully down the bank and step over the lingering puddle from two days before Sunday, a brief spring shower. I stand at this newer post and slowly find a barb and gently prick my thumb with it. If I squint I can see the nearest cows. Red and white faced. I smell them again and also the flowers on this vine that's creeping up the newer post. "Elegants," Mothermae said they were. I said "elephants," and she laughed and shook her head and wrote it on a piece of scrap we'd gleaned.

Today is the second day after Sunday; two days since the

priests had their hands all over me. On the fifth day I'll go to the grate and see. Again I feel the trickle of piss before I smell it.

"Voiture," I shout, and a calf near my hand bucks off out of my vision. I let the wire draw a prick of blood. Two cars close together. I hear it over Bridgett, the tires striking the metal plates. The boy on the crew falling the year after the water rose almost to this very post. But actually to the sign across from my house back up the closed dirt road through the evergreens, the pines. "Loblolly," the young priest says. But I don't say a word back at him, just nod because he crosses the prairie from Delios and lets me out a mile away though there're no houses there either.

"Lives up a side road," I heard him say in town at the mission, the front wall all glass looking out onto the street. The tables buckling under lamps and cracked leaf-green plates for sale. A white woman brings in an armload of folded brown bags. The two little girls with her all eyes and wrinkling noses, the tips turning red.

"God bless you," fat Father Stephen says.

"And you, too," she smiles to the old priest. The nun behind her silently shooing the girls away from the nearest table. The day's light caught up in a single blue bowl, its lip unevenly sheared off. Bringing the light up from its base, it burns along the jagged rim.

"Hey, you old fucker," they shout from the car. I tense my back, the piss smell stronger, a cow at my bloody thumb, in focus, her eyes unmoving, sightless; she chews her cud.

Once they never said anything. Then they said nigger, coon, blackass, words spit out windows. A can once struck me on the neck. Like the worst lick I'd ever got from Mothermae. Why, I don't remember. I remember always minding. We'd "scour the neighborhood," as she called it. "Oh, look at what this is," she'd shout at me. "Oh Milton, they've lost this for sure. Fell out of the trunk. Child tossed it out the window."

Once there were two shoes, the same set. They fit her until I had to rip the toe out. Her feet beginning to fill up with gas. The hay I scattered on the floor—the hay Rudy, his friend, no one ever came back for—to ease the shock of her steps. "Nope, I'll just stay put here. You go out." The year I went out alone; the year she was sick but got better for a while.

Before the creek sign business. And long before that boy on the road crew painting the railings fell off the bridge. Head turning to me as he sprawled past the mulberry bushes I sat behind. He opened his mouth and I felt my own open wide. But we didn't know to speak or scream, and his feet hit the top of the steep bank and pitched him perfect onto the rock that's always above-water unless it's way out of banks. "It only has two speeds. Low and flooding," she'd say. "Dry or wide open."

Later I waded out to the rock carefully. Already an old man. And looked up. Then I lay down on it and looked up. There was the railing like a thick fence and the evergreen boughs and the hairy tufts of swallows' nests. Like warts or moles up underneath the bridge, blotching the pale smooth concrete. Sprouting from the icy shadowy concrete. Rocks are always warmer.

"Get your mind offa that stuff," I say. "You silly old man." I'll just have to get me more faith. Woke up to spring this morning. Three days after Sunday with the priests. One Sunday a month in town with them. The young one full of chat, picking me up, driving me back to the empty line of loblollies. This morning a blue jay came into the room through the smashed panes. They never came back to feed the hay. The front rooms finally collapsing under the weight. Mice and rats chattering all over, still too cold at night to leave.

He flies up in the dark above my fogging breath. The Holy Ghost. Mothermae made us kneel around the bed. Me and two sisters and brother Willy. "Baby Jesus," she always launched out, her voice like a knife in the dark room. I imagined the white baby in Mary's arms turning his head to hear. His baby's face blank and not very helpful. "Baby Jesus is many colors," she told me after my two sisters had left and Willy had been shot to death somewhere so far off we never knew the reasons. Or if it was even the truth.

Were we precious in his sight?

All the years of priests—since I first went into Delios to get her a doctor but didn't; it dawning on me standing in front of the mission that she really did want "to go to her reward," as she called it. They were always harping about Mary. They only sometimes mentioned Jesus. The older, fat one, Stephen, more than his young helper.

Yesterday I rose late and got only as far as the newer fence post. Today I'll push these old bones hard and get on up to the Farm Road 3941 sign. I brought home a hubcap that says Oldsmobile on it. And a mangled tin cup I'll straighten out with the hammer from the year the boy fell.

That'll be fine to do. The jay woke me early enough. And what did I hear yesterday, up ahead? Those were buzzards fighting over something. I'll take the shovel out by the garden. I remember the onion sets the young priest put in my Sunday box, "the gift box," Father Stephen called it. "We've heard so much about that garden of yours, Willy. Maybe this year you'll bring us some homegrown vegetables, okay?" I nod and look at the floor at my newest tennis shoes from out of another of their boxes. Fuck you, I think. Fuck your years of boxes. You don't even know my name. Or where I live, a mile past the loblollies toward Monterrey Prairie 8 miles, the sign says. I nod and reach out and take Father Stephen's hand. Fuck you white priests. I nod some more and turn, thinking of the grate, that it's also once a month, five days after this Sunday in Delios with the two priests. "Don't hurry," I whisper to myself as we walk to the car. Then there's Mothermae's voice as I sit, holding the gifts in my hands. I was waiting for it.

"Milton," she'd muttered in my ear that night. She hadn't taken the time to light the kerosene lamp. And I realize how in my house now there are no light switches or plug-ins because it was built before that. I've always smelled wood and kerosene in the air. That is the smell of light to me. There's a smell to sunlight across the hay that wakes me slower than a loose jay frantic along the warped ceiling.

"Hurry, Milton, and get dressed." Hurry up to leave that other house I can't remember. To walk for miles in the dark to the town and the hospital to see him large, always the color of a deep mud hole. The white sheets flung around him like snow in a Christmas book I could already read back then.

Next he died. The sawmill gave her some money and we moved soon. In with some relatives. The children outnumbering the adults dozens to one. Then somewhere else; losing, on the way, Willy and my two sisters. We walked up here one summer. We had walked for miles until she just turned off the road and lay down on the grassy ditch bank. "Milton, you find some place. I'm done in. Just done in."

"Have you ever had a job? Paid in Social Security?" the first priest, the red-headed one, asked me years ago. Ran out of the mission, caught me turning away. Minding Mothermae who begged me not to bring a doctor. He pulled me in off the street, his woman's fingers on my coat. His eyes on the trinkets I'd pinned to my jacket. Which are pretty and for good luck because they come to me as gifts off the road. On my lapel I probably wore a piece of ribbon. The tire gauge like a heavy silver pen in my pocket. I shook off his thin long fingers. Too much. All of them asking, wanting too much. From now on I'll beg two boxes, have to come in only one Sunday every two months. With spring there'll be food enough. Next winter maybe I'll try to hibernate like the frogs along the outside rim of the well, jammed together, packed tight in the wide cracks in the crumbling brick wall.

Now I pull on my jacket, put my hand on the pressure gauge, and remember the white man in the long black car. He was the color of lemons under the dome light. I could see better then. The stars just above where the yellow stripe begins at the curve as thick a dusting as I'd ever seen. I stood perfectly still across the road as he got out in the cold. I heard his teeth chatter. He said, "Shit, I'll never get there. Goddamn cheap tires." And I heard the sneeze of air from the gauge and he reached back inside to turn off the headlights. I heard his zipper go down and I smiled as he pissed a heavy stream on the pavement. He stood over the broad asphalt patch. The sound was muffled by it. Finished, he pulled his dick several times and had trouble packing it back in, zipping it up.

Then he looked around and over at me and in one complete motion he opened his door got in started up tore off, the door slamming on its own a long ways down the road, his almost flat tire burrowing up the soft asphalt.

The next day I sat on the gravel shoulder and reached out carefully to pry the gauge out of the road; I patted the scar closed with my palms.

Now I leave my hand on its scarred barrel, the tiny plastic stick of numbers broken off in the patch. It told me then the best way and not their way though I needed the food soon after Mothermae died and I had spent the last of her money neatly folded in the bottom of the saltine tin. The real way is to keep your mind off of Baby Jesus and all the priests' prying questions. Think of what's really happened in front of your own eyes. Like the man giving it a couple of extra strokes in the middle of the country. The stars only inches overhead. I hate I scared him off. I'm glad he liked that stretch of road. "It's full of lessons," she'd say when we were old together and felt like husband and wife. We never slept apart. For comfort and warmth. "Lessons all around." Somehow she meant Baby Jesus lessons, but I had always doubted that. Beginning the moment he turned on the bed and let out the longest lowest rush of air I have ever heard. "He's gone," the white man in the white coat had said to the long full ward. Everybody listening to the noise and the statement. But I thought, where's there to go? He's not here and wouldn't be home or filing saws at the mill. And I doubted if he'd ever been here at all. Been at any of those places. Jesus wrapped up in it all. The priests over the years trying to add Mary as another complication. As if the more things involved we can't possibly see the better.

Again I'm getting a late start; just like yesterday. I wash my face out of the bucket at the well. All around the house things are blooming. The pears and plums. I take what's left in the bucket and drizzle it through cupped hands on the lettuce, the little plants the color of the young priest's eyes.

"How old are you?" Father Stephen had asked the year I was sick off and on. His hair jet black back then. The mission lunchroom steamy, outside the town of Delios empty storefronts taped with silver duct tape. I shrugged. Fuck you, I thought. And besides, I don't know. Sixty. Ninety.

They continued to get their hooks deeper in me. Father Stephen's hands clasped like plaster praying hands over the sheets of paper. Like the cupped hand I keep on the windowsill.

They drove me to a doctor in Brantley Cove. A small young black man. I almost said something when we were alone, but I saw his face in the mirror as he washed with green soap. Later his fingers barely touched me, gingerly along my throat and at my chest and shoulder blades. The shouts of nigger, whistling foaming full cans of Budweiser, Schlitz, which I finished off, everywhere around me. I always stand stock-still like the cows, surprised it's come back to this again.

I don't build a fire in the stove to fry the bacon they gave me that I keep in an old metal bicycle basket deep in the well. The wires icy to the touch. Instead I take some of her ribbon off the nails near the back door. Two yellow ones which bring with them a laugh of hers about something or other.

I tie them in my beard, let them dangle on my chest. The yarrow has begun to spread near the door; I try not to crush it as I get down on all fours and pull out the twisted shovel with the shattered handle. As I walk down the road that circles the house and goes down through the evergreens that block it from Farm Road 3941, I smell the jonquils. And I want to let Mothermae listen to my mind thank her God and Baby Jesus that it's warm again and I've come out of the cold to see the road, to "glean it clean," she'd say. Glean it. *Glean* a word I believe sprouted from black bottomland cotton fields. A word I love.

"No, I never worked. My legs never been right." And we looked at one another until he smiled and nodded. "That's all right. That's all right."

So I lied, Mothermae. Okay, you smiling, compassionate man, I walked into Hopkins when I was twelve and she cut across Mecham's Prairie to Luxor to mend clothes in a converted garage. I could read. I sat for centuries in the dark filthy room. The old man droned on and on. Stomachs growled all day. We all itched lice. The dark, near the muddy floor, under the desks full of mosquitoes drinking constantly, raising purple welts. Spring thunderstorms melted the cardboard windowpanes. The damp curled paper.

Later I came with her past the windowless garage to the sawmill icehouse. In the awful August heat I loved the wet sawdust floor, the blocks of ice warped and irregular rising to the ceiling. The clunk of metal tongs, the shower of ice from their deep bites.

Nigger this, nigger that. The oldest, who ran the hand-cranked crusher, named Nigger Boss.

But soon there were troubles. The whites laid off and waiting for someone to cuss, to yell at from store porches and through screened doors.

No work for anybody. The cross-tie mill burned. We woke that night smelling it on the dry wind and walked down to the Farm Road—just dirt then, the scant gravel beat to the sides—to watch it. The sky free of town lights. It was wonderful and Mothermae shook her head and cried. Took my arm and trembled.

Somehow she worked on. She saved almost all of her money in a metal saltine tin.

I never went to see the destruction. Now there were shootings all over. Whites drunk and mad. Black folks trying to be absolutely quiet and still in Shady Bend, the nigger quarters down the hill from the icehouse.

No work. The last time I saw the icehouse, we walked through its empty dark caves, me and Boss. "I'll be okay. You, too," he said more than once.

And so I tried this and that. For a long time we drank whatever we could find. And some nights I'd stay in the quarters with someone from work.

Now at the ancient fence—a few rotten posts, the rusty wire sticking up from the pine needles like some red leafless vine—I turn away from where my road goes on to cross the bar ditch and connects with Farm Road 3941. Instead, using the shovel as a cane, I move slowly through the saplings so I'll come out onto it a long ways from the house. My ribbons flutter in the slight breeze. I ease across a low spot and cross another abandoned road. I stop to breathe but I don't sit down. That day I'd been on the road until after dark. I crawled up this slope and sat listening to them in the car. The windows were down. They rocked its stiff springs. She kept saying, "There, right there. No, right *there*." But he didn't seem to be getting it right. He shouted "Nancy," and the woods came back with its sounds of frogs, an owl far away along Bridgett Creek.

They began again. Something I could never do. Only once and I melt away to sleep. The small house in the quarters full of people noises and the heavy odor of kerosene and boiled supper. She called it my dick. What I'd thought of as my thing, what Mothermae had called it when she washed me in the metal tub we'd gleaned from somewhere.

We fought and drank and sat on the porch. And everything else, I guess. Years ago. She'd drink the whiskey we got in Mason jars and at almost sunup she'd hit me with her fists as we lay on the bed. I'd jerk awake, the others beginning to get up. Coughs and the last deep snores from the soundest sleep. "Goddammit," she'd shout, "I can't even sleep. Why can't I sleep, you bastard. Laying there snoring. Get out, goddammit. Go on home to 'Mothermae I.'"

"Nothing turned up yet?" Mothermae'd ask. And I'd shrug and walk back into Luxor to drink and sleep with her. With Kay.

Until I couldn't anymore. When they burned most of Shady Bend down. Black and white. And Kay just sat on the porch, drinking, and never let the jar touch the floor. Hugging it between her thighs.

I stepped over one of the white bastards outside of town. Someone had laid him out cold, a brick propped against his temple.

But I don't count any of that. So maybe I didn't lie to the first priest or later to Father Stephen and the thick heavy Jesus, now a grown man, on the wooden cross on his vast chest. "No, I've never had a job." Besides, all that was before Social Security shit.

She still sewed. Up to the very end. And I complained about my back for years until one day I just stopped in the middle of the sentence because both of us were tired of hearing it.

People came to me over the road. I gleaned the road.

Like now, when I come up out of the ditch, deeper here than anywhere else except at the grate where it drops sharply into the creek. That's tomorrow. I admit I've pushed it up a day. One day only. That's bad enough. I won't do it again. Never have before, that I can remember. I can't begin to be haphazard now; I'll miss something valuable.

Today the clouds are low. The gray light is warm. The asphalt is damp though there wasn't rain last night. Along here once a car ran off the road and rolled through the fence—the posts, metal now, were spindly cedar then. I heard the whump of it all from the house.

No one was killed. Or even hurt. Back then the road was slow and the cars heavy and strong. I helped two white women up the bank and we talked for a long time until a delivery truck for a meat-packing plant stopped. We shook hands and waved. I heard the wrecker at the car the next day, but I didn't go look. I already had a pair of earrings and leather gloves which I wet and stretched until they fit.

Today it's a raccoon. Sometimes it's a possum or a dog or tabby cat from somewhere far off. Or maybe they're let out here by people tired of the trouble. Once I helped a man chase down a beautiful red bird-dog who'd escaped when he'd stopped to take a piss. He'd given me two dollars and a can of beer from a yellow cooler he had on the passenger's side. He asked about something I had on my jacket or in my hair and I think I told him all about it. And he asked more and I saw he understood everything I said.

I dig good and deep. The raccoon whole, not a sign of broken skin anywhere. Those are the best kind. Before I nudge him in with my toe, I squat to look at his face. His teeth are exposed in an even line. Tiny and sharp. Locked into either a snarl or a grin. And I consider Mothermae's opened mouth and the man I stepped over once leaving Luxor. At this point I always worry about dying and not being buried at the house with her, up under the pears. If it's not sudden, I could go to the priests. Or lay down out here with a note pinned to me. Or maybe just stay inside with the birds banging into the walls.

This morning I rise before the sun and bring up the bacon and light fat pine pieces in the stove. There's bacon and one egg from the priests and a handful of chicory coffee in the pot of rolling water.

"Silly old man," I mutter, eating at my table made out of a door. But I still don't think much about the grate or my silliness about it—my making it into some big deal which it's not. Instead I get up and gently pry out tacks with my thumbnail and take the ancient yellow pieces of paper and sit down in the open doorway; beyond my feet the new dark green mint running in all directions like crazy. And though I don't lift my head still heavy from sleep, stiff from the cold nights and warming days, I think beyond the scraps. "Bruno Hauptman Executed." We've had that forever, huh, Mothermae. I watch her hands take it down. Putting it back, she matched tack and hole perfectly. "State Rep. Wallston Convicted." "The Eagle Has Landed." Sometimes some of the story. Never all unless it's there right on the back. In the gift box they put pamphlets and tracts. About Mary mostly. Seldom about Baby Jesus grown old on Father Stephen's chest. Never God himself, I think. But sometimes the green-eyed younger one slips in a *Reader's Digest* or, once, an almanac.

I have read those. Looked at the pictures. But these from our walls are the best. I remember where I found this one about white men on the moon. It was the year the drought burned up the garden, the pears dropping easily, still the light green of mossy places in Bridgett Creek. As hard as stones.

The year white men landed on the moon. I imagined I could see them that summer. But black folks would have showed up better, I laughed. Like periods in the newspaper. Like ticks on the white face of a Hereford in the farthest pasture up the hill from the grate, the road going on to Monterrey Prairie 8 miles away. There there were black folks, white men, too. But I've never been that far. The white men on the rising orange moon closer than those at the Prairie.

Today I'm anxious to get there; too anxious maybe. I know I've cheated; I'm going a day early. Once a month. And I thought about traveling there once every two months and right now my mouth's dry as can be.

I hurry myself up. I wash my face, put back the bacon, ignore the sprouting lantana, the first white veins showing along the buds of the tea rose. Though I walk down the road trying to recall its fragrance. "Milton it's wonderful. Milton, look at what you've found us," she'd said, me pulling her up the road. She stood about here and looked around but I pass on, walk through the memory. Don't stop to look back. Pears. Tea roses. Sometimes the recollection of Rudy's strong body all over the place. On the porch. The sounds of hay lifted up, thrown down. For years we thought maybe this spring they'll remember. Or this winter the feed will run low. If they come, they'd come across the field where the road crosses a dry stream and edges around a hill. But they never did. Rudy on the moon maybe.

Now I ease across ditches, enter sapling thickets, emerge on the road as the sun comes up behind clouds pink and orange. The bridge, the hill ahead blurred, washed all together, a dark sweep to the west. The sun on my chilly back. It'll get stronger.

That first day was terribly hot for late summer. I thought of the icehouse. I remembered Kay. I had forgotten the porch and the whiskey; the smells of Shady Bend.

Mothermae was dead, but the boy hadn't fallen to the rock yet. Sometime in there, in between whatever the in-between is. I try to keep it all straight, but I don't think I can anymore. It's like something has worn out. But I could see better at least. Terribly hot but no drought. The thunderheads came on late in the afternoon, at almost sunset, their bottoms blossoming red like roses, the lightning like the day's sun. There'd be some rain. Not much but enough to give things a drink, a sigh of relief. I was walking, expecting that later.

I had never crossed the bridge. The sign peppered with holes. I stopped there, put my little finger gently in the holes, saw the jagged exits. Thirty feet to the rushing water, green like young lettuce. The road going uphill on the other side. Sharply up into thick evergreens and gone over the top toward Monterrey Prairie 8 miles.

"Just stay away from it, you hear me? That's going too far. It's full of water moccasins and greenbriers anyways," she'd said. Some fear, respect, darknesses in her words I understood but didn't, too.

So we always turned back the other way. Seldom gleaned up to the creek. Only sometimes, if we spied something shining in the sun. Something of interest.

Now I cross it. Without fear. But that hot day I must have been breathless. Like I was stepping on the moon. A nigger on the white face. The green water below boiling around the large flat rock. Then there was the car. Voiture. I heard it ahead in the evergreens the other side of the hill and I ran toward it, past the other sign full of holes and dropped down the rough concrete along its side, my skin scraped away. The swallows' nests over my head, my feet sticking through a mulberry bush.

The car come and gone. Only its sound present. Clanking over the metal plates, air rushing through the railings. I must have been old even then.

Now the best path is the easiest. Cross the road, hang onto the sign with its wrong name. Swing slowly until my shoes touch the headwall. Drop two feet and walk under. A natural path here. All the way to the mouth of the grate. The outlet of a drainpipe at least four feet in diameter. The hole set back at an angle into the cement, rusty iron rods the size of my fingers broken, bent upward, trapping whatever comes down from beyond the top of the hill.

I sit and lean back against the concrete. It is damp, still cold in the shade. I wait a moment. I wait even longer.

That past day not magic, not Mary or Baby Jesus. Though she would have said all that. And she'd looked at me as she often had. Her eyes drawn almost shut. "Behold the lilies of the field," she'd say. "The birds of the air."

The niggers of this land.

But it was close to magic, I guess. Everything coming all at once.

I laid against the grate, my hands all scratched up and beginning to bleed. I sat up slowly and looked up into the black hole. There was a mound of leaves, paper, metal shining, all of it dried into a wad of stuff. I crawled toward it but before I reached out the voices came to me over my shoulder.

"As pleasant a way as I know."

"Better than anything, I'd say."

A woman's and a man's. Then laughter. And I see myself gasping for air like when the wind howled down the stovepipe and smoked us out into the open.

Angels, Mothermae?

The sounds of them crystal clear and floating on the heat waves. Bright and distinct right at my feet. Passing through my head like a breeze.

But I'm not a believer, and so I scrambled past the tangle of greenbriers just in time to see them drift around the bend. In a long low wooden boat. A canoe. Their voices still coming back over the sandbars and the flat rock they almost scrape. The first and only time I've ever seen anyone for any reason on Bridgett.

White angels if angels, Mothermae. Angels with parasols and fishing tackle.

I turned around to glean the mess of rubbish, teasing out the tight bundle until I screamed, yelled, heard my voice for the first time in days, weeks. Louder than I've ever heard it before.

I beat it up the bank, heard it coming up after me. "Oh," it kept saying. "Oh, oh, oh," like great gusts of wind.

Below me the fingernails painted red, chipped, the hand crooked, pill bugs all over it, up against the grate, bundled in the tight dry weeds.

I held the sign; we swayed together. The sun right overhead for a long time. I thought of Bruno Hauptman, saw the picture of the baby they found. Stuffed up in a culvert like a parcel of things you ought to want to look at.

Now I laugh. Then I laughed too, later. "You're getting old, you goddamn sure are," I'd said. I begin to sort through this month's deposit. But there's been little rain to bring stuff down. There's nothing here, but I'm not disappointed. It happens a lot during the dead of summer. Once there was a whole book, its pages barely faded. *The Waitress Murders.* I still read it once in a while. Catalogs. Huge pieces of cloth that come in handy. I think maybe the bicycle basket came from here.

Now the heavy plaster hand is on the windowsill. I put a candle in its palm. It was probably from one of those store dummies. I love to remember that gray-headed man scrambling up the bank yelling. And after I'd had the laugh, I wondered if my voice had carried down the creek's channel to the people in the canoe. Had they said, "Shhh . . . listen . . . what's that? Listen!"

"My God, it's a person."

There's a chance all that didn't happen the same day, the day I discovered the grate. But I think it's so.

Gifts from God, Mothermae? Sometimes there are vague and distant noises. The rumble of thunder, the hiss of snakes from out of the mouth of the pipe. But it's not Baby Jesus turning his head this way, is it? Most likely it's a trick of the wind, or the pipe travels under a road, opens near some houses or a factory.

Coming out of the cold into the spring is the best time. I'm already thinking about planting some peppers. When I want to talk I'll go into town to the priests. I'll ask them about Mary, say I've read those brochures and they're interesting. Get the two of them really going. Or I'll take the shovel and walk down and dig up the asphalt patch. I've done that before. And when they show up in their yellow dump truck, I'll come the long way out of the woods without anything in my hair or beard. Sit and drink Pepsis with the black boys stripped to the waist and shining. They think I'm a hobo. They ask me questions about my travels that make the white foreman laugh and shake his head. I answer them as best I can.

FRIENDS OF BECCARI

August 3rd
Still on the banks of the Trinity

David Fisher
The Hotel Charybdis
Taormina, Sicily

My dearest Dave,

I'm sorry I haven't answered your last two letters, but much has happened the last six weeks. How are you and Marta? Here all seems well enough (only I'm suffering from the last month of summer heat). B. is relieved she's finished here with no summer session and, at Harper State next semester, only two courses. The children are fine. As usual, J. is still full of music and song; L. suffers from the imminent departure. She spends all day outside at play.

I wonder how the book on D. M. Thomas is coming? Only last night I decided to open the Old Bushmill's single malt, sit on the deck (next to the table crowded with ailing and dead bonsai—you were right, as usual, I don't spend the necessary time with the little bastards. And now, with the move in a couple of weeks, maybe it's best they all shed their leaves), and think of you. By the time you do get back—via Bolzano, Lake Como, etc.—we'll be settled in and the new place, new semester, new town (smaller but cheaper, I hope) will surround us.

Anyway, I sat on the deck and drank, missed our conversations, and realized I couldn't sit, drink, remain silent about what's happened though I don't know what to make of it all yet; though I think, in many ways, it answers a hundred questions we've asked each other over the last four years since you drove in from Phillips College and hated all the right things with a fine sense of humor.

I tried my best to drop it last month; I hoped it'd be smothered by the impending cross-country move. But somehow that only tantalizes it, provokes it. And your absence has me hulking through the department, unable to talk, everything quickly becoming even more foreign than it was the first time I saw it all. I know you'll understand.

Of course what our lovely writers do is fascinating, you know. Absolutely so. But it's not completely right because it does nothing to explain what I saw in Tegucigalpa. When we taught Poe, Dostoyevsky, Calvino, many, many others, we emphasized their distortions, bulging seams, oddities of time and place, repeated movements, sudden illnesses as exciting ways into the same old reality, some new way of exploring the same old human situations. They all just teased reality through a bit of illusion. Maybe the protagonist was insane and his madness gave him new insight or a frighteningly clear perspective.

Though the character is a murderer like Mathias in *The Voyeur*, he remains a man, and the world he distorts into repeating patterns found on beaches, tablecloths, suitcase linings is still an island the reader takes as real with sand, salt breezes, sea gulls. All these invented perspectives ways of seeing the same old things with vitality. Didn't we tantalize our students with the insights and outlooks of deranged men, ill men who reinterpreted the ordinary, the static, while we talked on and on in comfortable classrooms with hissing radiators and flaking paint?

It's method we admired, isn't it? New ways of seeing old dilemmas. But the world was always the world around them—a world of bridges over rivers, whores with tuberculosis—not something free-floating and amorphous with mysterious, unlimited possibilities. We certainly took comfort in that. In that, and in knowing, beyond anything else, that men sulking in dark cellars, writhing in nightmares, writing fantastic books were always men. Men as we understood them—even in madness, even as murderers.

We cagily, with great ease of mind, told our classes there were only a dozen themes available, all the rest is brilliant variation. We were smug, weren't we? But none of this explains my brother and Odoardo Beccari.

I'm sure you remember how often I've spoken of my brother. I know, when I wrote you last, I mentioned how he'd taken off on an old-style world tour in the spring. His was the biggest success of the Clarke family. Where I never "quite got through with school," as mother quips, his was a meteoric rise. After high school and the Navy (anything, he said, to escape the late '50s) he finished college at UT, then went into the state legislature while in law school, etc., etc. Now, at fifty, he's a hell of a criminal defense lawyer in Patroon. Remember we once talked about the Hopkins case—the papers termed him "The Beast"—and how my brother turned down the offer to defend? But those are the sorts of cases he's taken since losing his bid for state prosecutor general back in '74.

For years he had a tremendous impact on me. He was the first person in our family to go to college, almost assuring I would, making my own children's education a certainty. He'd get me to memorize and recite Kipling poems when I was six or seven and he was home on furlough. We love one another in the typical Clarke fashion—nothing demonstrable at all. Tight-lipped, hands in pockets, expectations present but unspoken.

But over the last few years there's been a change with him. It's so noticeable even my mother has commented on it, though she's put it down to absence of familial responsibilities, etc. Approaching fifty is dreadful, I'm sure (and you know better than me, right?). With him it's made for a certain restlessness and listlessness simultaneously. It's almost (and here's where I'm sure we discussed him as an example) proved our point that one drifts into conservatism because it's less complicated (offers a clear right and wrong view, good and bad), seems the natural outcome of age and its subsequent tendency to withdraw and avoid contact with what's ugly, complicated, and sorry in the world.

Anyway, without children, he's poured himself into the law, and in it, I think, he's passed from some idealistic desire to help the unfortunate to a dwelling on the unsavory character of his clients, their melodramatic and awful plights; most of all, on their refusal to accept the consequences of their actions. His politics have gone from McGovern to Reagan and beyond (he holds some absolutely horrific views on personal freedoms vs. the state's power, etc.). I know we talked all about this when we discussed some of our colleagues, whom we dubbed "The General Staff." And we noticed that almost axiomatically, as compassion lessened, stature and bucks grew. So did feelings of disappointment, isolation. Now the naive and youthful worldview was something to be embarrassed about like a vestigial tail, an open fly. They were grownups now and only children saw things without wise cynicism.

Sorry I'm drifting, though I wanted you to recall what I've said about my brother and what we together have said about the way the world's turning lately. Now, quite unexpectedly, I'm afraid I may have an answer for such stuff.

Here's the important point of all this; the simple but mind-boggling thing which outdistances all our lovely writers who altered the man and the world in ways we could understand and accept, indeed applaud and admire. What the Friends of Beccari can do is something utterly fantastic and profoundly disturbing.

Allan wired me from Tegucigalpa, Honduras, about six weeks ago. He sent me airfare with a cable asking me to join him for a week or ten days and saying we'd fly back together. B. was a bit upset at the whole idea of, as she said, "the boys getting to play," but she didn't really mind. She and Allan have never gotten along very well for all sorts of reasons, and besides, her father was ill with his prostate again. So, she chided me but was finally eager about the trip. She and the girls decided they'd spend the time at her parents', easing her mother's duties.

He'd left four months earlier, closed down the office, let the secretaries go, and simply slipped away without an itinerary. Mother was dismayed at the immaturity of it all. I was delighted because I realized he needed immediate relief from his job. And, I suppose, I hoped he'd mellow his cynicism somehow and return some sort of optimistic liberal as he'd once been when I was in high school (In the state legislature, he'd authored bills broadening the state's pitiful social services). Anyway, he'd once been my hero and I wanted the best for him. A trip that'd provide him with whatever he needed. Though I guess I foolishly believed he only needed time alone in some exotic place to shake a fifty-year-old man's summing up of things. I honestly don't know what I really expected to find in Tegucigalpa, his last stop before coming home. I never once thought about those Kipling poems he'd made me memorize, or his romantic view of the military (even, honest-to-God, after four years in the Pacific with the Navy!). All of which had been given to me too, a legacy from him. But I'd stopped with it years ago through Sassoon, etc. Though I readily admit it can still fascinate. Why else do I so enjoy *The Raj Quartet*, all those ancient Bengal Lancer movies? Now it all wells up and frightens me because of the possibilities.

Anyway, he wired that he'd arrived and I flew from Houston to Tegucigalpa. I'm not a good traveler, as you well know, so all the way I was disoriented, fearful of foreign languages, saw myself as homeless, unable to eat or drink in comfort. Stepping out of the plane, I encountered the unruly crush of hundreds of people. Though it was cooler and less humid than in Houston, the tropical sun seemed sharper, closer.

I had the address of his hotel, but out in front of the terminal, standing before one of a hundred battered Toyotas, was a shabbily dressed wiry fellow who rushed up to me with a sealed envelope. Torn open, it revealed a note from my brother, though hastily written (I guessed then) because it was his handwriting but not clearly so. In it he told me to stay with the bearer, who'd bring us together.

Four hours earlier I was in traffic on the way to Houston Intercontinental, but now it was all different—just off-key and foreign enough to exclude me without fascinating.

I have few impressions of Tegucigalpa. It seemed full of cars and the staggering vegetation of tropical places (though Florida's my only true reference). All the time I was rereading, refolding the note. I had no expectations really. But I had thought we'd meet in his hotel, have dinner, etc. And though this was hardly upsetting, it was unexpected enough to worry me.

We left the city, at least its center, and wound up a hillside and turned abruptly into an almost hidden driveway—a brass plaque and opened, heavy iron gates blurred past. Here was a wide pearly gravel drive traveling even higher up the hillside until it ended in a small parking lot full of expensive vintage cars. As I paid the driver, who remained in the car and passed my light bag out the window with some difficulty, I heard the sounds of powerfully stroked tennis balls and splashes into water, though neither court nor pool was visible through the thick but well-manicured trees and shrubs.

I relaxed a bit under the wide archway of the front door. This could be anywhere, I thought. San Francisco, Houston. And though I also realized its sumptuousness—beveled glass panes in the heavy oak doors, muted carpet, and the glimmer of brass in the vestibule beyond—I'd really only seen such in magazines and movies.

The doors suddenly swung open and, as I'd been whisked through the city, I was now rushed into the paneled darkness and glittering brass. The liveried Honduran spoke quickly and too quietly for me to comprehend as he took my bag in his left hand and my elbow in his right. There was some sort of central hallway. In one room off it there was an incongruous fire blazing dramatically in a magnificently manteled fireplace. In another, farther along, the high walls were crowded with trophy heads, their glass eyes sparkling in the dismal light. Jerking my head around and pulling against the man's grasp, I managed to slow us enough to see two youngish men standing near the far window of the room next to the fully erect trophy of a gigantic brown bear, its paws aggressively outstretched. I sensed they turned to look my way, though we hurried past. Here, muffled by brocade carpets and tapestried walls, our feet made no noise. Somewhere, far off, or close at hand—it'd be impossible to say—there was the click of billiard balls.

This is too perfect, I remember thinking—trophies, tall angular men, billiards—when my silent guide stopped, set my suitcase just inside a door, and gently pushed me forward as if I were a bashful child. And certainly I was worse than that at the moment. The two-hour roar of the jet engines, the frantic taxi ride, this perfect movie set—all of it coalesced in my bowels with a sharp stitch of pain. I felt the sweat on my forehead, and I staggered a bit in the gloom and reached out to steady myself on a table edge, rattling some immaculate arrangement of delicate cups on pale lace.

"Are you all right, Donnie?"

I turned to the doorway, but the Honduran was gone, the suitcase at my feet. Allan stood across the room silhouetted by the French doors.

"What's wrong?"

The gas pain relented after a moment, and I straightened gingerly and crossed the red-and-blue Persian rug to the French doors, the only source of light. Beyond them I noticed one end of a tennis court. On it a thin man expertly returned the white ball. He was dressed in a white shirt and white, long pants. Surprised at the costume, I realized that the two men standing by the bear had had on some sort of uniform. Scarlet-and-black tunics of some sorts.

"Donnie, answer me. Are you all right?"

His back to the light, Allan took my hand from my side and squeezed it firmly. Sensing my confusion, he acted the guide now and carefully placed me in one of the two high-backed leather chairs that faced one another over a low mahogany table. The French doors to my left allowed in dull green light filtered by the luxurious vegetation.

"Donnie, how are you?"

Looking up at Allan's voice I looked into the face of a total stranger. I must have said something because, half-rising in protest at all of this, the man rose too and took my shoulder and firmly pushed me back into the chair. I rose again, heard myself sputtering words of complaint. Who the hell are you? Where's my brother? What is this crazy place? Everything came tumbling out. And all the time I stared into the lean angular face and blue eyes, the chin strong as a rock, and listened to the voice soothe me in tones I thought I fully recognized but, just as quickly, didn't. I realized this man's accent was foreign, clipped, most un–East Texas. But here and there it was surely my brother's voice, the tone from childhood when once he'd purposefully thrown the softball at my head, the rush of blood from my eyebrow terrifying him more than it had me. The boy's voice of concern, responsibility, fear.

"Donnie, old Donnie," the tall, graceful man kept saying, his beautifully manicured hands on my knee and arm. "It *is* me. Don't worry. Everything's fine. Everything's really quite grand." Again, the frightening accent strong in places, the soothing tone present nonetheless. The most unsettling thing I know—the deceit of the normal, the expected.

I wiped my face with the heels of my hands merely redistributing the grime of the last few hours.

"I've come back to tell you something. Are you listening? Donnie, will you pay attention?" Now there was irritation in his awesome voice. Irritation at me, my inability to stay with things until completion. His chiding I used to cringe at. You'll never learn that way, he'd say. His own hands deft, his own patience often worn thin by my ineptitude. He spoke louder, and the Honduran quickly appeared behind his chair. He gave clipped commands, the voice completely foreign. His accent most definitely English.

"We'll have coffee, all right? Then I'll tell you something." Dismissing me, he turned his face toward the French doors.

What do I do? I kept thinking as I watched his face. Should I run screaming for the police? I must have moved again, perhaps straightened my legs from under the table, because the man looked around, and, for the first time, the light outside brightened and fell full on his face.

"Allan," I shouted, my voice ringing the cups by the door. His hand again on my shoulder, I looked into a face that matched the disquieting voice. He'd favored my mother most; his face a bit plump, his chin fairly strong, his cheekbones hidden, porous skin scared by severe acne when he was a teenager. But in this man those most familiar features had blended with others. The chin was more pronounced. The skin softer, more finely grained. The entire face gracefully elongated. The pale blue eyes of my brother were now cobalt.

Perhaps I actually did faint. There is some brief gap here filled with the sounds of distant voices. Then, quite suddenly everything was happening again as if someone had simply adjusted the volume and picture. There was a cup of coffee in my hands, and I drank the strong liquid.

Dave, I know I've taken too long getting here, to the point. But you'll understand why in a moment. You've known me for years now. You know my smallest defects. I'm a poor sport and a bad player—an embarrassing combination. I've been unfaithful to B., and you, the man of principles, have never once chided me. I drink and clutch my enlarged liver. You've understood my own feeble writings and bolstered my often flagging career. I'd never do anything to cause you or anyone alarm, grief, upset. I've written this damned letter a half-dozen times. I'm not frantic now; I don't think I ever really was. I finally flew back to Houston and went home and lied to everyone. Later I drove up to his office in Patroon and went up the stairs to his apartment above and rattled the door. He's left all of that behind like a discarded carapace, a shed skin.

Jesus Christ, this draft's no better than any of the others.

I drank the coffee, my hands trembling. It wasn't a conversation. Allan spoke, his face, as it moved in and out of the light, like his voice—a mixture of my brother and things foreign, graceful, sophisticated.

"I've come back to tell you," he began, refilling my cup. "I wanted you to understand, old man. Thought you ought to know." He grinned, his teeth long and straight, no chip on the left incisor from my pushing him, at the age of fifteen, off the foot of our parents' bed.

It was all monologue. He didn't expect me to respond. Soon into it, he grew still and looked out the window. His awesome voice in the quiet tone one uses for moments of passion, terror, or despair.

My own thoughts jumbled and choking. Listen, I had to keep telling myself. My bowels rumbling, hurting.

Allan didn't mention Odoardo Beccari for a long time; he didn't take the long, thin book from his jacket until later.

Instead he issued a torrent of invective. His usual complaints even more harsh, bitter, unyielding. He ranted about the blacks at home. But it's the same all over, and he waved his long fingers in exasperation. The country gone to hell. The liberals still thinking everything's valuable and worth saving. Such disgusting concern for the puny and weak. "By God," he kept saying, "what's a healthy, strong white man to do?"

The diatribe grew stronger, more vehement. He quickly passed the point where one could dismiss it all with some offhand remark. I'd argued with him a thousand times, you know that, but now he was so utterly different. He seemed stronger, more sure. He said things we've all thought but known to hide if we can't extinguish them entirely. They were black, cruel ideas spoken by a tall, graceful man in a mellifluous voice.

His whole body quivered with excitement; he stood and began pacing in front of the French doors. Outside the tennis court was empty.

Where had all the pride in country and race gone? Who'd given the world all the advances over the last thousand years? Even before. Savages, weakness, moral corruption. Womanish-men. Mannish-women. The world gone topsy-turvy. He'd seen it from his trip; he knew the world. Poorly run governments. He let it all loose in bursts of words.

Such a burden on some of us, but a burden we had to shoulder, he said from behind me, his beautiful hands on my shoulders, his sweet breath on my ears. Betrayal, he said. That summed it all up. But the British had tried, even the French. Not the fucking Spanish. Look at their goddamned legacy worldwide. Everywhere now they're only small people with minds full of crap. Soft, useless children.

"But I came across this." He took a book from his coat pocket. "This and the friends of Odoardo Beccari." He sat heavily, his face florid and contorted; he slapped the book on the table. "Here . . . it's all in here. All we need. And many of us," he waved his hand around, "have found it. Here. But in Malaysia first, you see. God, was I lucky they found me. At the hotel, old sport. They knocked on the door and I let them in and they were full of the answers I'd been looking for. We're all looking for. We've just started here. You should see us in Southeast Asia. And India . . . well, there's a starting place, eh?" Allan laughed and sat back and talked. My dismay grew. I'm certain my own face reddened; sweat dampened my collar.

I never could figure the book out. I hoped you might. I thought of you, after I'd taken it. But later it disappeared. Stolen back, I think, by the Friends of Beccari. And I went to our so-called library, too. But there was only his book on the botany of Borneo first printed in 1904. Later I met Bob Finley, the guy we liked on the Curriculum Committee, at the Faculty Club and mentioned Beccari to him. He's in anthropology and knew a little himself, but remembered a travel book by Redmon O'Hanlon he'd read two summers ago, and it filled in a few more details. From O'Hanlon's *Into the Heart of Borneo* I learned about Beccari's pro-Lamarckian, anti-Darwinian position; there was only the briefest mention of his idea of "plasmative epochs," the secret of which the Friends had somehow manipulated, formulated, practiced, preached to the select like Allan.

But there in Tegucigalpa, in the private club of the Friends of Beccari, Allan told me the gist of it all though he was wrung with emotion: once in actual tears; shortly thereafter, in chuckling delight.

He was born again, in the truest sense. You see, in Beccari's hypothesis a "plasmative epoch" allows for every living thing to adapt more easily to external conditions. Certain stimuli can alter form. Beccari even allowed, it seems, for the possibility of conscious alterations. Creative evolution. If dogs, Beccari wrote, had associated with people during such an epoch, they'd be talking. Dreams, he wrote, are simpler than Freud would have them. They're recollections of previous plasmative states. Beccari's own frequent dream of flight was, to him, nothing more than his own birdness from a distant plasmative state altered yet again by a later one.

Allan clapped his hands in delight, his voice familiar and foreign. "You see, it only remained to figure out if such epochs could be orchestrated, predicted, arranged. Really all we learned was how to coax them along. A few rather difficult calculations. Some rare natural ingredients . . . nothing artificial!" He wagged his un-Allan-like, graceful finger at me that had once been as pudgy and short as our mother's. "No drugs." He nodded and leaned back.

I opened my mouth but didn't speak. Only my legs were working. My feet, under the table, crossing and uncrossing.

Allan laughed loudly and talked on about the Friends of Beccari and their grand design to "change things back a bit," as he put it. Politics, religion. Abruptly, he returned to his vehement attack on society. And, just as quickly and firmly, I believed none of this was true; it wasn't really happening, or, if it were, someone, maybe my real brother, Allan, just outside the door, was having a tremendous laugh at my expense. This private club wasn't anything to be suspicious about, the book at my knee could be anything—a volume of Jane Austen, an old company ledger—and there were only regular things around, things of this world: servants, billiards, tennis, a swimming pool.

Here I was, alone, in Honduras with someone who only vaguely favored my brother as, perhaps, hundreds of people do. And all this absurd Beccari stuff. You want to be this? Read a book and . . . what? Wish? Add and subtract? Take peyote? Join our secret society? Conspiracy, plot, the convolutions of the late twentieth century. I was deeply confused. I'd left Houston only five hours earlier.

"Look at India," Allan was saying calmly. "Christ, what a mistake to let the coloreds have it. What would it be like if we were still in charge, old sport? Just think of it!" Then, there was a low voice from the door and we both turned to see the same liveried servant who'd brought me in and, behind him, two military officers in uniform.

"Ah, ha." Allan smiled and stood. "I'll be back in a few minutes. These Americans," he nodded toward the doorway, "show up for strategy sessions now and again. Several of our chaps are really quite something in military ops. Me, I'm plodding along. Sadly it's necessary these days. Nothing'll come easy, I fear. Anyway, we're glad to oblige. Those bloody 'Nigger-aguans' are giving us hell." With a pat on my shoulder, he went through the door and they walked a ways down the hall. I could still hear their mumbled voices.

But I paid little attention. Instead, without a single completed thought, I stood and put the book in my pocket. Edging quietly around the table, I took two steps and opened the French doors. Again, I didn't pause to think but crossed the lawn, passed the empty tennis court, and intersected the gravel drive near the gate. The whole way, from the doors to the street to a bus stop down the hill, I imagined the tall angular men standing at the French doors watching my descent. And one of them was most certainly my brother, Allan, his hand on the shoulder of an American Army colonel. The look on his face the old look of disappointment. You've no patience, he'd chide. Where's your self-control?

You know me, Dave. I'm a mediocre scholar, a better-than-average carpenter, someone who's meticulous about income taxes, my children's education. So you know I didn't run off into Tegucigalpa in shambles, in the state of one of our young protagonists—feverish from starvation, in a rage over money, gasping from the final stages of tuberculosis. True, I was terrified at what I'd done by taking the book, my mind running in highest gear. Downtown I stepped off the bus in front of a hotel, and realized I'd left my suitcase in that room near the door. Fortunately, I had my traveler's checks and passport in my coat pocket so I managed to check in. Later I hurried out, away from the book, and bought a couple of shirts, some underwear, and an inexpensive nylon overnighter.

But I was distraught, dismayed. Fully dressed, I sat on the balcony, the city noises of Tegucigalpa the same as everywhere else, only the smells really different. Harsh, animal, uninhibited by rules or regulations.

The book was impossible to read. It had been cheaply printed, which didn't help. But even had it been perfectly legible, it was mostly equations, formulas, diagrams of islands or amoebas—I couldn't tell which. And where there were written passages, the words, though English, were in some meaningless combinations of code. Here and there someone had underlined a series of numbers or a phrase. In the margins there were interjections, I think, but those too were all scrambled.

The first night I awoke with my new pajamas soaked through, and, in the dark, I groped my way to the flimsy bureau and searched out the book and took it to bed, pushed in far up under the mattress and realized, by my action, something I'd kept quiet and secret from myself—they might come for this. Early the next morning I flew to Panama City.

But all this was thought out, you see. It wasn't really panic. I was worried, I admit. The more unintelligible the dirty yellow book, the more unsettled my peace of mind. And besides, I simply couldn't come home five or six days early, could I? I had no plans at all about what I'd say to B.

I toured Central America, I guess. Though I didn't pay much attention at all to San José or Belize. I spent most of my money in airports, hotel restaurants. The last couple of days I spent the good part of the day bent over the book, searching through its pages again and again, drawing on cheap hotel stationery the figures, diagrams, copying the passages. I needed to understand what was happening.

The last night, under the weak yellow light in the dirty bathroom, I inspected my face, jerked closer to the glass, my heavy breath fogging it, to stare at my lips. I didn't think I'd ever looked closely at them before. Now they seemed foreign. I moved them, mouthed a dozen crazy phrases from the Friends of Beccari, and waited. The water dripped in the stained lavatory; a phone rang through the thin walls. My lips moved again, but this time I spoke out loud. "Jesus Christ," I said over and over. Just look at yourself.

I flew back to Houston the next day and landed in an afternoon thunderstorm full of heat and dazzling flashes of light. I stood a long time at the baggage carousel until I realized my suitcase had passed me several times. But it wasn't the nylon bag full of dirty underwear and shirts wrapped around the book. It was the leather suitcase the liveried servant had put just inside the door. You know, I didn't even open it. The weary customs official waved me through and later in the car I just sat for a long time. The rain whipped across the parked cars in vast heavy sheets. I practiced making up stories. And decided to write you whenever I could.

That night, with B. at my shoulder, I laughed, grinned, talked loudly, my voice ringing around me and her and the children. The happy traveler had returned. No, Allan decided to stay. I unlatched the suitcase and, on top of my unused clothes, there was an array of souvenirs. Beautifully dressed dolls in native costumes; silver earrings for B. and, for me, a heavy mosaic, tesserae depicting some ancient Mayan ritual full of animals, bizarre men, the smoke of incense rising from stubby pyramids. Everyone talked at once.

I'm sure you've noticed the enclosed clipping. It's from the *Houston Chronicle* about a week ago. Though it's a bit hard to make out, what caught my attention were the white officers leading the Indian troops across the bridge. You know, it's the old trouble in the Punjab with the Sikhs and here's the second Gandhi making the same mistake his mother did of storming the Golden Temple in Amritsar. But anyway, that there were still Anglo officers made me examine it more closely and, though it's pretty damned fuzzy, I'm almost positive the white officer yelling—the one who has lost his helmet and is half-turned to us—is Allan. Allan and those Friends of Beccari insinuating themselves in India again to lead the "coloreds" out of their own childish mistakes. There and elsewhere in Central America, Africa.

A couple of weekends ago I lied, said Allan'd phoned me at the university, and I drove up to Patroon.

It was a scorching day, there'd been little rain in a month. I thought about you much of the trip. And about what we'd said often—the world growing more callous, frighteningly racist again. I composed part of this letter on the drive, wondered what you'd think of my revelations. I guessed you'd believe me. I'm calm in my new misery. My despair isn't clinical in its proportions. I know I hoped you'd offer some answers. Though what's there to say, I wonder? It's one thing to fight those ideas in your opponents—political, departmental, community. There's some hope, even if it's distant, of changing minds, altering viewpoints. But the Friends of Beccari *become* all those antiquated perspectives full of avarice, repression, distrust. Now the world steps back when, as we believed, it was just barely in the light. What will such western chauvinism bring now, at this late date? Can't you see awesome numbers everywhere adopting it, clinging to it as the stained yellow book alters, regresses. The gibberish of numbers, diagrams, paragraphs offering the romance of antique order, control, clear-eyed white faces again in charge, the deferential, obliging masses hunkered down, their own good in all our minds.

I parked the car in front of the beautiful limestone building. The ground-floor office was locked. I squatted, opened the mail chute with my fingers, but there was no jumble of mail and all I could see were thick carpet and dark table legs.

I climbed the stairs at the side up to his apartment, but the door was locked and the expensive glass pane was frosted.

I sat for a while halfway down the steps waiting for something to happen. But what did I expect? Allan was something else. The cicadas sang in the heat. I figured I'd get a phone call some day soon. And a voice like theirs would tell me my brother was dead somewhere too far away for me to retrieve his body myself and that he, the perfectly modulated voice, having developed a close companionship with my brother, would take care of everything. Not to worry, old man.

I sweated on the steps. Then I stood. The apartment and office abandoned carapaces, cicada hulls, reflecting the perfect outlines but empty. My brother was Beccari Man, the newest-old manifestation. Dave, do you think there's anything we can do? Whose responsibility is it, if not mine? Is it yours, too? Ours? I picked up one of the empty hulls, gently parted it from the wooden railing and held its weightlessness in my palm. From all around they pelted me with their triumphant cry of terrible release.

Awaiting your reply,
Don

BACKYARDS

Richard put the groceries on the table and walked back to close the door against the summer heat. For a moment he breathed deeply and inhaled the fishy odor he'd noticed yesterday, the second day in his brother's house. And though he'd looked for its source, he hadn't found it.

Tom, his only brother, had begged him to house-sit the month he and his wife, Megan, would be in Chile on a faculty summer program. "It'd be great," Megan had said over the phone. "You'd get out of that damned Houston in July. What's the humidity there, 98 percent?" And she'd laughed. Her laugh convinced him. That and the unexpected realization he was tired of Houston and the one woman he'd slept with in the last five years and she only recently; a new assistant accountant at work. Their recent months of sex becoming tangles of clothes because of her impatience. And once she'd bitten him on the forearm. After she was asleep, Richard went into the bathroom and examined the purple wound for a long time. Then he slept on the couch, waking often to watch the door to the hallway, afraid she'd come through it, her teeth bared. Now, though the wound had disappeared, he put his finger to his skin.

At the last minute, Tom and Megan had left early in the sort of frenzy Richard should have expected from his brother. It was very much like him to have gotten the dates wrong or the plane tickets or something. Richard was sure that was why Megan had phoned with the news, her voice layered and deep—the only woman's voice he paid much attention to. He hadn't seen them in over two years—since the Christmas the ice storm had rushed into Texas fiercely and killed the power at their parents' house, bent pine saplings almost to the ground. There'd been candles and kerosene lamps—the old days for his parents—and quilts on knees and early bedtimes. A lot of looking out of windows into deep gray afternoons.

Coming from his bedroom at the front of the house, he'd seen Megan naked in the mirror in their bedroom. She was alone, at the window, her fingers slightly parting the blinds. She hadn't heard him. He stopped on the cold oak floor amazed. There had been few women in his life, none before his second year in college. And he'd never seen such a sight before. The demanding woman in Houston was nothing like her.

Richard had flown to St. Louis and taken the bus two hours to the northwest. There'd been a manila envelope in the mail chute with door keys, instructions about appliances, a pad of signed checks for incoming bills. And a brief note from Megan saying she hoped he would enjoy the slow pace of Coalston. She jabbered on so about mental health and locating our centers that Richard wondered about her own well-being here in a town a long way from Denver, where'd she been born. And besides, hadn't they both just escaped to Chile? Richard couldn't imagine such an impetuous action. It was hard enough for him to make it from Houston. He was much like his father, who'd once been offered a high-paying job in Europe but couldn't leave the piney woods of East Texas he'd adopted as a young husband.

But what had he done his first afternoon in their house? Richard shook his head. He'd taken a shower and tried to get beyond the memory of the Houston woman lying on the couch and asking him to play rough with her. Then he'd thought about the few women he'd seen naked, Megan in the mirror. In high school there'd only been hands, opened blouses, sweating windshields.

Unhappy with the soft mattress in the guest room, he had taken his suitcase into their room and dropped it on the beautiful quilt he recognized as his mother's work. He opened their dresser drawers; he opened the closet, pushed back clothes, poked through shoe boxes, found a snub-nosed revolver in one and felt as if he'd found cocaine. This wasn't like Tom at all. Then, Richard smelled Tom's strong and spicy colognes and, in the third bureau drawer, put his hands into her underwear. Pulling out a fistful of panties, he scattered them on the bed.

For an hour or more he went through everything he could. He told himself that here was a chance to piece everything together—an opportunity to know them both better than he ever could any other way. Far more complete than what one learns over telephones, from infrequent letters about the superficial details of health, money, parents, work. Tom was his brother and Megan his sister-in-law. But their lives were secret and foreign, and here, suddenly, he had the perfect chance to find out who they were.

So he took out things, examined them, put them back, fighting, all the time, his conscience, guilt, amazement, the fear of being caught by their sudden return. Their faces in the door of the small study dumbstruck at Richard sitting at the desk, rummaging through old bills, lecture notes, memos concerning the League of Women Voters.

My God, he kept thinking, what am I doing? I'm the most secretive, private person I know. How would I feel? And he saw himself returning once from the kitchen and finding her with a book she'd taken out of his bedside table. He couldn't comprehend such an action. He had thought then how he'd have to keep an eye on her.

"Jesus," she'd said, oblivious to her crime, "you keep this sort of thing in the bedroom? Wow, everything there is to know about junk bonds."

But he hadn't stopped himself. Not until a folder had buckled and spilled across the floor, and, bending down, he'd read the medical expenses for artificial insemination at a hospital in St. Louis. They were enormous, and evidently the college insurance didn't cover them. There were several angry letters from Tom to the insurance people and one from Megan, less angry, her approach one of quiet logic.

Richard sat for a while, completely convicted, and then he had straightened up and unpacked in the guest room and drunk a large glass of sherry from the serving cart in the dining room.

That night in their bed he listened to them talk about him. My poor brother Richard, he could hear Tom say. He doesn't have much of a life there in Houston. Oh, he's perfectly fine. He could hear Megan's rich voice. But his life really is mostly work, work, work. He's always been that way, you know. And Richard winced at Tom's voice and, for a while, was glad he'd gone so drastically out of control and had searched their house.

The next morning he'd woken to the fish smell he'd been unable to locate and now guessed he'd just have to get used to.

In midafternoon Richard was interrupted by a series of sharp raps on the front door. He laid his autobiography of Henry Ford on the end table and got up from the couch. Out the big bay window the sky was cloudless, the leaves on the maples along the street drooped. He knew how hot it was; this summer was defined by drought and crop failure throughout the country and, in the west, tremendous forest fires. At night, on the news, it looked as if the whole nation was hot and weary.

When he opened the wooden door, he looked down on a short, broad woman in her late fifties, her hands full of brochures, small plastic bowls, flyswatters. Richard shook his head. "I don't live here; the owners are away."

The broad, moon face broke into a smile, and she came up the steps and under Richard's arm. "Of course you don't, honey. You're Rich, Tom's baby brother. Bet it's hotter in Houston now, huh?" Her lime-green, shiny dress was all reflection and motion as she laid the items on the coffee table and dropped heavily onto the couch. "Whew, it ain't no picnic here, is it hon?" And she wiped her forehead and chin with a handkerchief from her huge purse. Richard smelled the sharp bitter lemon odor of perfume as she clicked her bag shut.

"Barbie Glass," she said, leaning back to look up at Richard. She patted the couch at her side. "Have a seat, Rich; I can't stay a minute you know." She shook her head. "Can't leave the old man alone these days. You know how they are."

Richard sat and nodded his head. He looked through the window, but there wasn't a car anywhere. He realized she was a neighbor.

"Anyway, Megan and Tom told me all about you," she reached out and patted his arm. "Big-time accountant, CPA," and she rolled her eyes. "So, how's little ole Coalston shaping up? I'd have come over earlier—saw the taxi out the kitchen window," she twisted herself around. "That's us—me and Buddy—right over there. But I thought I'd give you a day to get settled in."

Richard turned too and nodded at the small brick house with green, mismatching trim.

"Anyway, it's an old people's neighborhood, you know. Tom and Megan the youngest in a dozen blocks. And we all love 'em, the honeys. You're a lucky man, you know."

Richard nodded.

"Anyway, here's the Welcome Wagon," and she rolled her head back and laughed loud. Richard laughed too and looked down at the coffee table.

"Really, I'm one of two of us. Me and Julie Hutchinson," she wrinkled her heavily powdered nose. Her eyes were small and the depthless blue of water in a swimming pool. "So, I thought, I'll leave Buddy just a minute and meet Rich and why not take him the usual, huh? Why not?"

Richard nodded and smiled. And Barbie went quickly through the assortment of pizza coupons, bottle openers, flyswatters—from a funeral home. "Can you believe that?" Barbie cackled. Richard said he couldn't. She rattled on about the quality of the schools, troubles with the few blacks who were ruining everything in the county, the weather, the nearby lakes.

"Well," she said, and stood up surprisingly quickly for so large a woman. "Buddy's missing me for sure by now." And she reached out a hand that Richard, puzzled, met to shake.

But instead, Barbie grabbed his wrist in a cool grip and led him through the living room to the adjoining dining room that opened onto the rear deck. She brought them close to the large sliding door. Richard looked out with her. Barbie's finger jabbed the glass.

"You'd better watch out for 'em." She stared up into Richard's eyes, and he felt compelled to nod.

"Who?"

"There, in that mess of a garage apartment, the green one—right there."

Richard hadn't taken the time to sit on the deck yet. There was no shade, and the planks and metal lawn chairs looked scalding in the harsh sunlight. Now he took time to notice the house at the end of Barbie's finger.

The backs of all the yards ended in a wall of dense woods that lined the banks of an invisible creek. The lawn to his left was manicured; he'd seen the old thin man who lived there mowing at noon. The house to the right was a bit closer to the street than Tom and Megan's. And, obviously, the owners had built some sort of garage apartment, or perhaps had sold the back half of their large lot. The faded kelly-green house was unusually dilapidated for this neighborhood. Its gray roof buckled in several places. A low fence of raw cinder blocks surrounding it was almost obscured by high weeds. Abandoned pieces of rusting machinery lined the fence. There was a tangle of scaffolding and a cement mixer with a split bucket. It reminded Richard of housing in some third-world country—poorly planned, hand-built, unfinished.

"Oh, I know Tom and Megan love kids . . . and who doesn't? But they'll come to see when they get back. They'll learn. Those kids just moved in a few months ago. Parents never home and they've run amok. You oughta hear Buddy," Barbie chuckled. "'End of the world,' he says. 'Barbie, they'll be the death of me.'"

"Bad kids," Richard said lamely.

"Oh hon! I mean, they've just moved in. Before it was vacant a year—property's hard to sell these days—and before that just Mrs. Clemson until she kicked the bucket. Didn't realize it for a few days, those sorry kids of hers. And it was August, too."

"What's wrong with them?"

"Just been a mess," Barbie shrugged and walked back to the front room, pulling her purse up on her shoulder. "We've never had anything like it here. Most of us have called the cops on them at least once. They steal things—newspapers, lawn ornaments, Mr. Eaton's three-wheeled bicycle, we think, and wrecked it where the creek crosses under Helena Road over by the fire station. They smashed Madge's herb vinegar she was steeping on the porch. Now the Bentendorfs say they've caught them in their garage sitting in their new Buick. And later found nails all in their aluminum siding. But what can you do?"

Richard shook his head. "I don't know."

"Well, Rich," Barbie whacked him hard on the shoulder, "just watch out for 'em, huh? And if you need anything, Barbie and Buddy are right over there twenty-four hours a day. We never go anywhere . . . and seldom sleep. It's a geriatric neighborhood, all right," and she chuckled and waved a fleshy arm over her shoulder. Richard watched her cross the dry, hot yard. Looking down at Megan's zinnias bordering the porch, he decided he'd water and maybe even trim a few of the wilted hedges late in the afternoon, though Megan had written him about the young college student whom they'd hired to take care of the yard. Yard work was something he'd seldom done since he lived in an expensive condominium complex in Houston and had no yard and couldn't possibly say who his neighbors were.

Friday morning, a day later, Richard sat up in bed and screamed, his voice rebounding off the walls. The face at the window disappeared.

He sat there and collected himself, breathed deeply before he swung out of Tom and Megan's firm bed and looked out the window.

It was almost midmorning, the beginning of another endless

summer day. The sky was already a milky haze; the bush below the window was dying from the drought, dropping yellow leaves as if it were fall.

A young, thin boy streaked around behind Tom's metal storage shed. Then another child, a girl fifteen or so, leapt over the low, weed-covered wall and ran after him.

Then another girl, a bit small, but also blond, burst through the back door of the garage apartment; Richard could hear her yelling. It was high and shrill, full of real fear. She had a sandwich in her hand, the bread flapping open at every step. Right behind her came another boy, terribly thin and redheaded.

Richard opened his mouth, rapped on the glass. "No," he said. "Stop it." And, not taking the time to grab his bathrobe, he rushed through the quiet house to the rear deck, still damp in the shade from the dew.

Now he heard her scream, high and awful, as she scrambled over the cinder-block wall and crossed into Tom's yard. Like a pirate, her red-haired pursuer put the butcher knife in his teeth as he raced up the pile of scaffolding, jumped into the high grass, and emerged like some attacking animal.

"Hey, stop it!" Richard pounded the wooden railing. He didn't know what to do. He looked at the green house, hoping a parent would intervene, but the torn screen door sagged halfway open.

In the middle of the yard, the girl stopped, turned, and flung the meat-and-bread sandwich at her brother, who stopped too, stuck the knife in the ground at his feet, and glared at her.

"You sonofabitch," she said, taking in gulps of air.

The redheaded boy squatted and pieced together the sandwich. Carefully he wiped the grass off it onto the knee of his pants and then took a bite. He spoke with his mouth full. "Fuck you."

Richard was appalled. He felt trapped in the balcony at some terrible play. Again he stared at their house, the opened door, the black mouth of it. Some yellowed sheets and underwear hung motionless on a clothesline.

He'd never liked children, never wanted any of his own. Neither had the biting woman in Houston. "Little shits," she called them. And, for a moment, he admired her, wished she were here to witness this.

"Hey, you two," he shouted, and they turned and stared at him. The boy reached down and pulled up his knife; the girl shaded her eyes from the morning sun. Richard looked at them but didn't know, now, what to say. He wished he'd stayed inside; he realized he was in his pajamas. He recalled what had woken him and turned his eyes to the metal shed. He saw two heads duck back around.

"You two come out from behind there. Right this minute." He spoke in the office voice he used on subordinates who'd caused him inconvenience.

But they didn't come out. Instead they laughed loudly.

"Kimmy, Chip, come on . . . hurry," a girl's voice coaxed. And, in a flash, the redheaded boy and girl were gone.

"Stay out of my yard, you little brats," Richard shouted at them.

"It ain't *your* yard," the older boy's voice answered.

Richard listened to the sounds of their feet and bodies scurrying through the underbrush. Turning to go inside, he stopped and moaned. All along the porch, where Megan had placed pots of flowers, were clots of wet dirt and shredded plants.

Richard sat on the deck and drank a freshly made old-fashioned. It was too dark to read any longer. He laid the opened book on Peter the Great on the wire end table.

Next door they'd been making noise since sunset, but, out of principle, Richard hadn't paid attention. Now he watched them come in and out the battered door.

There were no lights on in the house. The older girl had a flashlight. They worked like ants, passing one another, pausing for a second's contact—a shove, a pounded shoulder. "Ouch." "You're asking for it." "You sissy." "Little piece of shit." "Bastard."

They were loud, oblivious of the neighborhood. They brought out a folding table, straight-backed dining-room chairs, paper sacks.

All of a sudden, with an orange flash, the older boy had lit a fire on the ground.

They yelled behind their low wall and gathered closer to the fire, their faces yellow flickering masks. Richard noticed Kimmy, the sandwich girl, wore glasses.

He thought about how, in the city, he didn't live near children. And, in the malls, he paid them little attention except to sidestep them and their mothers.

Beyond the wall the fire died down until the older girl poured something on it and it erupted, causing them to scream with excitement. Then they began to sing, or maybe it wasn't a song but a poem or chant of some sort. It was less melody than rhythm. He couldn't understand the words.

In bed, before he slept, Richard parted the curtains. There was only a flicker of light; the house still dark. He thought he saw their shapes sitting on the chairs. He was sure they'd used the fire to cook their supper. He'd smelled the odor of meat. On the edge of sleep he wondered if they had electricity.

Then, after the memory, everything happened quickly. It was as if everything else was waiting for Richard to recall something he'd never really forgotten. It was early afternoon and he drove under the carport after a late lunch at the Golden Corral. Coming around the corner to enter the house from the deck, he stopped and edged closer to the wall. He felt like a spy as he cautiously looked around the corner. The blue-and-white police car was parked in the apartment's driveway, and the officer stood by the opened car door. The children stood in a semicircle a few feet from the patrolman, whose lips moved and right index finger wagged. But a hot rising breeze obliterated his words. Richard watched him pull out of the driveway. For a moment the children stood transfixed, and then they shouted one long gleeful shout and scattered in four directions, hopping over upturned bicycles, screaming over the fence.

Richard thought of his own youth and his "country relatives," as his father disdainfully called them. But this memory had never been cloaked or forgotten. Richard thought of it often, maybe once or twice a year. For him it was an emblem, a definite lesson, the clearest illustration in his life of why he was Richard, this thirty-four-year-old man.

His mother's cousins were all great sportsmen; they fished and hunted whatever was in season. And he loved visiting in their houses on holidays because they were all full of energy. One wall, in the oldest cousin's house, was devoted to guns—shotguns, pistols, deer rifles. There was the foreign and raw smell of bourbon on Christmas afternoon. The men laughed loudly as the women cleared the table. His mother joined in cheerfully; she loved the convoluted familial gossip. But his father sat silently at one end of the wagon-wheel couch coddling a bottle of beer. Richard watched him nod and smile and knew, at fifteen, how foreign all this still must be to his father. It was the South to this man born and raised in Milwaukee.

So Richard tagged along as they visited barns, hung on fences to watch stallions mounting frightened mares. Sex, he couldn't help noticing, was all noise and unwillingness.

They had dozens of calico cats, black-and-tan squirrel dogs. None of the cousins minded horse shit or kennel smells. They wore scarred boots; he and his father borrowed rubber Wellingtons. Slipped them on in a tack room full of saddles and bits, smells of grease and leather.

After he'd begged and whined for weeks, he and his father joined the cousins early on a mid-November morning to squirrel hunt. Already they smelled of whiskey. His father looked drawn and pale, his hands tight around the barrel of the borrowed shotgun. Tom, who was away at college, had never been interested in these people; had never made such demands on their father.

The woods were frigid and silent. They all shot squirrels; Richard watched his fall thirty feet into the mouths of the dogs, and he was amazed at their eager violence. A cousin his own age grinned and waded into them, smacking heads with a gloved fist.

Before noon, one of the cousins sang out, his voice echoing up dry creek beds, and they all converged on a huge snapping turtle the cousin had dragged from its winter home under a fallen oak. It was awfully old, the elderly cousin said. Its high-domed back was obsidian black and spotted with patches of green, live moss. The closed flaps protecting its head and feet were orange. They all admired the turtle until one cousin bent over and put the muzzle of his shotgun to its emerging beak and fired. Then the others stood back and did the same until there were only pieces of shell and flesh.

Richard and his father neither fired their guns nor looked at one another. Later, on the way home, his father called them savages and Richard decided to abandon them. He turned back to his family and their quiet, solitary lives. He had always felt himself lucky; he figured few people had such clear opportunities. Of course it wasn't only that one moment in the woods, but it had been a telling event, had become a powerful memory. And, over the years, he didn't think he had embellished it at all when he occasionally took it out and examined it like a valuable jewel.

The sagging apartment door banged shut; Chip, the red-headed boy, howled like an animal. Near the pile of scaffolding, the two oldest children kissed passionately; Richard wondered how they were related.

He wouldn't deny the allure of their lives. Even after he'd gone inside he thought about them and returned to look out at their house. He felt he was blushing; his forehead was warm to his touch.

So, in a couple of days, the children returned to the yard to play. They made-believe using the storage shed. And Richard watched them from the couch until one morning he stepped quietly out onto the deck and cautiously sat in a webbed lawn chair.

Chip looked up from his howling game, his fingers dug deeply into Tom's drought-wrecked grass, and watched Richard. In a moment they all fell silent. The older two came out from behind the shed, their faces blushed and drenched in sweat. Richard almost turned his head away.

They formed a tableau. All around them sprinklers clinked and a hot breeze rattled bamboo wind chimes.

Richard stared at them. It's all right, he said to himself. Don't worry. I only want to watch. Everything's just fine.

The older ones spoke quietly to the younger, and they sat together in a circle for a few minutes. Then, like a football huddle, they touched hands and shouted, resuming play.

In a day's time they had captured Tom's backyard. Richard watched them work like ants carrying from the garage apartment broken chairs, bicycles with warped wheels, headless dolls, sacks of clothes. The two oldest—the boy stoop-shouldered with pale eyes, the girl with just a hint of breasts, her nipples hard under her tight T-shirt—wrestled and wrote things on sheets of notebook paper. Like sibyls they paid no mind to them afterward, and the scraps, driven by the hot breezes, plastered the base of the house, flew to catch in other people's hedges. One night, after they'd retired behind their wall to gather around the fire and cook, Richard collected paper until his back ached. Sitting down at the kitchen table, he looked through the damp sheets at the stick figures in sexual positions he'd never imagined. In some there were stick-figure policemen surrounding houses, bullhorns to lips. In all, the houses were repetitions of the green garage apartment down to the low wall, the scaffolding, the split cement mixer. In one, a redheaded child hung from an upper window. In all of them there wasn't a single scene indoors.

One morning, with his coffee in his hand, Richard emerged to find the two youngest digging furiously with a spade. They'd already crossed half the yard with a shallow trench, the grass uprooted and turned over.

"Hey, you two!" Richard placed the cup on the railing and stepped down onto the brown grass. But Kimmy only turned around and grinned, her teeth yellow and snaggled. "You shouldn't do that," he continued, but Chip didn't break his rhythm. Instead, without glancing up, he tossed a shovelful of dirt in Richard's direction.

"Now listen here," Richard said, and stopped ten feet from them, his clenched fist outstretched. Then he dropped his hand and looked over at the dark sagging door of the apartment.

Who are you? he started to ask. What is all of this?

Instead he went inside and, from the couch, saw them fill the narrow ditch with water from Tom's unrolled garden hose and begin sailing pieces of wood down it. Soon all four of them joined in and dug a second canal at right angles to the first.

All afternoon they romped in the water and dark mud. The older girl's neck caught the sunlight like gilt, her eyes downturned to the toy boats. The older boy taunted Chip until they fought in the trench, clawed and bit and screamed.

Kimmy ignored them and put the dribbling hose into her mouth until her cheeks ballooned. Soon they were all yelling, tearing through the neighbors' yards, and Richard went around to the side and turned off the water. He noticed that their sailing boats were pieces of painted clapboard siding ripped loose; in some the bent nails were still shiny.

Some mornings they were out by the shed. Once the two youngest were on the deck drinking Dr Peppers at seven in the morning. Soon he began cleaning up after them. He filled the trench, patted down the friable grass. He scrubbed the crayon markings off the deck planking. He noticed he no longer opened his mouth to shout at them when they ran headlong into the shed and bounced off in one of their violent games. But he felt his face flush frequently, his head a bit dizzy as if he'd had too many cups of coffee.

But when he demanded of himself a trip away from the

house—to the store or a movie matinee—he could hardly wait to return. To sit on the couch in the infinite summer evening or on the deck and watch them howl and fight. The two oldest always touching—hand to elbow to shoulder. The yellow light warm on all their suntanned skins. The apartment door dark and sagging. He'd never seen a light on in a window. He quit reading his book by Henry Kissinger. At night he watched them at their supper fire, faces like masks but also the faces of children. Their motionlessness, rapt attention on the flames, a summation of the day's abandonment in passionate play.

On one of the rare days they didn't appear, but could be heard a block away in loud contests, the phone rang.

"What do you think you're doing?"

"Hello?"

"Just what do you think you're doing over there?"

Richard almost hung up. That's what you do in Houston, in the city.

"It's me, Barbie Glass. Remember, Rich? The Welcome Wagon lady. Your neighbors, Barbie and Buddy."

Richard nodded and looked across the street. He couldn't recall which house she'd said was theirs.

"Yes, of course. Hello, Barbie. How's Buddy?"

"He's the one made me call, Rich. He's mad at you . . . mad as a wet hen . . ."

Richard heard a thin voice beyond Barbie's; it was reedy and angry. "Sonofabitch," it said. "Sonofabitch."

"Hush up . . . shhh."

"Barbie?" Richard looked out at the houses. Two houses to the north a man sat on the porch in a wheelchair, but he didn't look toward Tom's house. Richard kept his eyes on him; he wore a thin robe over pajamas and spat into a handkerchief concealed in a palm.

"You're letting 'em take over. You're letting 'em overrun us, Rich."

Richard considered her words and found himself silent. The

man in the wheelchair turned his head to the door. There was a voice now behind Barbie's. Sharp, complaining, angry.

"They're ruining our neighborhood. Stealing mail, tearing up property. This and that. And we're old folks, Richard. And you're encouraging them. After we've tried to keep 'em in their own yard."

"Goddammit," the high voice shrieked.

Then he didn't hear anything; Barbie must have put her hand over the receiver. Richard imagined her small fat palm across his lips.

"What do you think you're doing, Buddy wants to know? Why ain't you with us, Rich? Look at what they've done to Tom and Megan's lovely yard."

Richard stared at the man in the wheelchair.

"Can't you help us, son? You seemed such a nice boy. Tom's younger brother, the CPA."

"Yes, of course. Of course I can, Barbie. But they're just kids, you know . . ."

"Bad kids, Rich."

"I . . ." And Richard hung up gently. He watched the old man on the porch cough convulsively into his palm, then he went into the kitchen and sat. He felt embarrassed for them all.

It was easier than he thought it would be. On Tuesday morning he went to McDonald's and bought a half-dozen sausage-and-egg biscuits and cartons of orange juice. He waited on the deck in the dew-dampened chair until they stormed out of the apartment and over the wall to the shed—its sides dented in places from their roughhousing.

"Hey, how about some breakfast?" he said in a stage whisper. The four of them seemed to ignore him. So, for a few minutes they continued to play with the collection of broken chairs, warped boards, and old chenille bedspreads and Richard continued to sit on the deck, his face warm as if he'd had whiskey.

Finally they came running and collected on the deck so close to him he'd stepped back and waved them inside.

That's the way it would begin. He'd buy sweet rolls or breakfast muffins. Or he'd fry eggs and bacon. After a couple of days they'd be cavorting on the deck, cracking the glaze of empty bonsai pots, picking at torn strips of webbing from the chaise longue, until he slid open the door and they rushed inside to the kitchen.

They seldom talked. They ate like wolves he'd seen on PBS. They jerked at their food, chomped down bacon, ham, and toast. Guzzled their orange juice.

They smelled like cat's fur—the smell of the sun on things that live out under it. Richard kept his distance, stood with his hips against the edge of the kitchen sink.

And then he let them play in Tom and Megan's house and they destroyed very little. All they broke he'd replace before the summer was over. There were dropped glasses, a bowl full of wax fruit—Kimmy took a bite from the Red Delicious apple and, in anger and surprise, pushed the whole bowl off the coffee table.

"Mista, you gotta dead rat in heah," Chip said, wrinkling his nose. "Don't ya smell hit? Somethin' wrong with ya nose?" He laughed, his teeth gapped and yellow. Richard saw they were his permanent teeth. He nodded, but he no longer smelled anything; he had gotten used to it.

But they seldom talked to him, and though they were soon into everything, Richard held his tongue. Kimmy and Chip found pots and pans in the kitchen to play with. He sat on the couch and listened to their wild babble; he heard them argue; they came to blows, swinging pots as weapons. Often one screamed and dropped to the floor weeping. But Richard just listened, knowing that if the pain were too great the child would run out the door and into the woods.

The oldest two played in Tom's study where there were dozens of old magazines and family photo albums. They typed on the typewriter and giggled. They lay on the carpet—Richard watched their feet stretched out across the doorway. Brown legs in the air, they talked a low foreign language, a dialect all their own. Sometimes, when he came from another room, trying to keep things a bit straight, he'd glance in and they'd be talking head-to-head and then they'd look up at him as if he were a ghost, their faces suddenly ashen and their lips drawn tight. He'd nod at them and smile, but they'd keep staring.

Some days they didn't come, weren't waiting for him on the deck. On those occasions he'd drive an hour into the medium-sized city and window shop and eat at some awful restaurant offering local dishes. Taking a mouthful of food, looking out the window at his brother's Toyota, he considered what it was he was doing. But not for long, and he answered everything with a shake of his head.

When they did arrive his breath caught for a moment at the top of his lungs. He sat on the couch in the living room and listened to all their noise—the crash of pans, the complaint of the abused typewriter. Standing at the back door, Chip scanned the yard with Tom's binoculars. That afternoon—they always left by two at a sharp command from the older boy, drawn to the sun—Richard couldn't find the binoculars. He wrote it on a piece of paper in the study, a list he had begun keeping. "Things to Do," it said, though it meant "things to buy, to replace." On the floor were dozens of sheets of paper black with typing. "Karen . . . Bobby . . . Hates . . . Kisses." A stew of typos. Odd pieces of themselves left behind. In the kitchen there were different traces. Puddles of flour, water, sugar. Cake pans full of soggy oatmeal. It took him more than two hours to clean up. Afterward he'd watch baseball on television until it was time to lie down and watch them around their fire.

"Holy Jesus, are you crazy?" The phone clicked dead. Richard looked across the street; behind him, the little ones fought. It wasn't, he decided, either of their voices. It was a low man's voice disguised as high.

The day the rain broke the drought, they stayed until almost five. Rising from the couch, Richard walked down the hall. In the study, with the rain pounding on the air-conditioner, the boy was asleep on the floor.

The girl was in Tom and Megan's bedroom. She wore one of Megan's Sunday dresses, the shoulders hanging down, the whole dress describing her young body. She sat on the bed watching the rain against the windows.

Richard stood in the doorway. The rain-filtered light darkened the bronze skin of her cheek and the backs of her hands. He thought about the rounder, mature body of Megan.

In the doorway he listened to the rain with her and, beyond her, to the snore of the boy, the sounds from the kitchen. He knew absolutely what he had known for years. He would never have children. He would never live like the cousins or these children.

One breast showed plainly through the thin fabric. It was hard, firm as a fist. She was probably sixteen; the rain-streaked glass softened her sharp girl's features.

Richard backed from the door, walked quietly past the sleeping boy, and sat on the couch.

Two days after the rain the weather turned cooler. Richard had straightened up and fixed himself a cup of thick, bitter espresso. He stood at the sliding door and listened to them in the woods. Later, he dozed on the couch until the sharp knocks on the flimsy storm door woke him.

"Coming," he said, and flipped on the yellow porch light. "Yes?" Richard opened the door and looked down on a huge man in greasy coveralls that gapped at every button, strained at the seams.

"So you're the bastard, huh?" The words slurred from thick lips. The man seemed as broad as he was tall.

Richard held the door open. The yellow porch light failed to repel the moths that fluttered and dipped in front of their faces.

"What do you want?" Richard let the door close a bit, but

with a surprisingly swift movement the fat man stopped it and laid a wide hand on Richard's shirtsleeve.

"You some kinda molester, that it? Bring the kids inside for *treats*?" He whined the last word and Richard smelled whiskey and realized several things at once.

"No, no, that's not it at all. Listen . . ."

But suddenly the fat man, his globular cheeks shaking in rage, his chin sagging like some brown animal's bloated throat, yanked hard and pulled Richard out the door onto the rough cement porch. Richard heard his shirtsleeve tear on the doorknob, felt his left knee flare in pain as it jammed against the wrought-iron railing.

The huge short man lumbered around on the tiny porch with Richard in his arms. A bear squeezing a foolish thin man. With a broad paw, the man would swat at Richard's face, and, working an arm free, Richard tried to protect his head.

Later, in bed, Richard saw it all from their point of view—as if he were at Barbie and Buddy's window. They never sleep. They probably had cups of coffee in their hands.

He touched his face where the man had hit him again and again with his ham fist. Then they'd fallen over the railing like in a western and plowed up the zinnias. Richard had yelled and yelled. He could hear his voice but not his words—he didn't know what he'd shouted.

"Goddamn molester. Kid fucker. Bastard." Over and over. With Richard shouting too, trying to cover his face, trying to wrench the horrible fat fingers from his collar, from around his arms.

Finally he'd hit the side of the house with a crack and, after a few minutes, all was quiet. First he'd sat on the steps and looked across at Barbie's. Then he'd gone to the bathroom and washed his face carefully and done all those things his mother would have done if he'd fallen on the sidewalk. Then he'd lain in their bed and considered everything and how he'd never been hit before and how he still had never struck anyone. He didn't sleep as such. Instead, in an aching doze he packed and repacked in his mind. Sometimes he discovered he'd included Tom's pants or Megan's shoes and he'd dump everything out and start over. Then he'd either forgotten to buy the airplane ticket or had put it in some pants pocket. There were noises, too, as if, offstage, other actors were talking too loudly about their own lives and what they were going to do right after the show.

The next morning Richard could hardly get out of bed. His neck and back were stiff; his wrists felt as if they'd been sprung. His face didn't look so bad in the mirror, though his cheek was as red as a strawberry and there was a purple bruise on his jaw.

He decided not to shave and fixed himself a cup of bitter instant coffee. He breathed deeply and inhaled a new odor, the pungent smell of leaking gas. But, sniffing around in the kitchen, he recalled that the house was one of those sixties all-electric models. Perhaps, he thought, it's Chip's dead rat. Richard imagined its corpse in some cramped, dark place.

He walked out onto the deck. The air was cool. He listened, but the woods were quiet. The only sounds the truncated songs of cardinals. Richard put his coffee cup on the railing and stepped down onto the grass that had greened-up since the rains. He looked across the backyards, left and right, several times as if they were a dangerous street he was about to cross. He imagined faces at all the windows, everyone knowing everything about him and the four children and the father. The memory of the fight caused his sore cheek to ache.

Richard walked across the yard, stepped over the sunken trench he'd inadequately filled in, and pushed his way through the weeds. He'd watched them return home; he knew the route Kimmy and Chip took. Clumsily he climbed the cinder-block fence and stepped onto the pile of scaffolding. He almost fell into the yard. For a moment Richard looked up at the faded green garage apartment.

He walked up the steps to the small wooden porch; his

pants leg brushed the ragged screen punched out from the door frame.

"Hello, anybody home?" Richard rapped on door. It felt hollow and rotten under his knuckles. He figured he'd apologize, say something to their huge father, so he could get them back.

"Hello in there, anybody home?" He didn't know their last name. "Kimmy, are you in there? Chip?"

"Wow! He gave ya some good uns, huh?"

Richard turned and looked down at Chip, who had walked around the corner. Beyond him Richard saw the other three emerge from the woods and sit on the dining chairs around the blackened circle where they built their fires.

"Your dad home?"

Chip came closer, stood beside the porch. He looked at the screen door. "Nope, he ain't never home." He looked up again. "He busted ya good, huh? Goddamned if he didn't." He grinned.

"Listen, why don't you come on over and play? I've got some new stuff you can play with . . . you and Kimmy. And we'll fix hamburgers . . . on the grill. We'll eat outside. How'd you like that?" Richard raised his voice and looked at the others.

"Are you kiddin'? Are you foolin'?" Chip jerked his thumb at the door. "He'll come home sometime."

"Listen, I know what." Richard stepped down the steps and looked at Tom and Megan's house. He was surprised at how it looked from this point of view. He stopped for a moment to examine it all. "What if you come over for a little while and help me look for that dead rat? He's really smelling today. He's stinking up the place real good. Help me do that, okay?" Richard turned and looked at the redheaded boy, who stared up at him and then clapped his hands, yelled at the others.

The three jumped up from their chairs and ran ahead. They all vaulted over the fence into Tom and Megan's yard. Yelling still, they pushed inside.

Richard stood at the fence and listened to them. He could

leave a note. But he'd have to go home for a pencil and paper and climb back over the fence. And he couldn't attach it to the door; he'd have to step inside. Besides, the father would know soon enough.

Richard climbed the wall and dropped to the other side. For a few minutes he watched everything from the cover of the tall saw-toothed weeds.

GYPSY MOTH

November 1969

I came from out of the field, over the barbed-wire fence, to the restroom door. Out of nowhere. Out of the blue. I looked back at the hill, the bare post oaks. Shitty night. I stamped my feet. Two cars on the asphalt circle of the roadside park. I hunkered out to them. A shiny red BMW. Black leather insides. The other an ancient Dodge. Rusted-out fenders. Tailpipe hanging low. Wired with a half-hearted twist of coat hanger. My people always give themselves away.

Later the old man grins. His tongue brown and furry from the Chesterfields. The stumps of his sparse teeth chocolate turning canary yellow at their crowns. I nod. I never smoke. He cackles. Grins. Winks some more. Stomps the pedal to the floor and the Dodge lurches, sputters.

I've never owned a car. A house. Only seen one movie. With Burt Lancaster. *The Gypsy Moths.* That's how I feel when I'm done and lay on them. Opening my shirt first and raising theirs up. In it Burt Lancaster wears these black stubby wings for the skydiving trick and he blazes down two hundred miles per hour, ears full of wind. His eyes looking right at me. That's the way I get. Pull my shirt out, hold it wide like moths' wings. Their eyes turning milky. The Gypsy Moth. Me and Burt Lancaster in a movie I saw in Rock Springs, Wyoming. The wind like an ice pick. The whole town perfect in the roaring wind.

I tell a story from my childhood to the old man whose dash

is crammed with crumpled paper. I like to tell my people stories. True ones. Pieces of me in exchange.

Mama had a cat that had no voice. It'd open its mouth wide and cry long and mournful. But no sound. Not the faintest noise. I'd pinch it hard.

On the back porch I punished it. Ran its tail under the rocker. All but break its gray skin under its gray fur. It'd scratch and howl and howl but the only sound was its claws on the linoleum.

I laugh. The old man looks in his rearview mirror. But I don't need to. I know he sees an empty two-lane road. November day gray like cat's skin. My people always look out on gray. On rain or low clouds like bruised flesh. Then comes the Gypsy Moth slamming through the overcast. The sun on its back.

TWO CARS ABANDONED
Pine Bluff police towed two abandoned cars from downtown. One, a red 1968 Ford van, was removed from a vacant lot on Biloxi St. The other, a 1951 Dodge, was found parked in an alley alongside the Tower Theater. Both vehicles had been stripped of their license plates. Anyone having information concerning these cars should contact the police department or come by City Hall. If unclaimed, the two autos will go on public auction the second Tuesday of next month.

August 1973

It's a fully equipped Ford Ranger pickup. I even found some money in the glove compartment. A twenty and some ones. It's hot outside in this little town, so I drive with the air-conditioner on, the windows rolled up. The cold air blasts my chest. I pat down my shirtfront. It's a brand new one and so are my pants—Sansabelt like football coaches wear on the sidelines. I've bought a new Stetson to celebrate, too.

Because I love summer. Everywhere. But here especially. It brings all my people out in the open. Now I don't find them just at the post office bundled up, noses red and runny. The funky smell of dirty rooms on them. By the tracks some negroes sit on upturned packing crates and slap knees and talk. And in front of the washaterias old frumpy women and thin ones in cheap cotton dresses lean against car fenders, sit on hoods, drink icy bottles of Coca-Cola.

People out, walking, clothes baskets on hips. A man sitting on the post office steps, tearing open an envelope. A woman with the hood up at K-Mart. I pull in next to her. She's in stretch pants. Her hips bigger than a mare's. Her face flushed, sweat dripping as she looks over her shoulder.

Together we do this, jiggle that. My voice geared to this weather so it's all open spaces and coolness and smiles.

Oh they love me always. And I love them. Who else does? I ask you. Who has the time for this young-old woman with red knuckles, grease across her chin? She hefts herself into my Ford Ranger, asks about the Yellowstone decal on the corner of the windshield. Something I haven't noticed but like in her. They're always wondering. They ask childish questions. They're poor but rich in spirit.

She thumps out a Virginia Slim. Her weight tilts me to the passenger's side.

I tell her all about Yellowstone as we drive across town in the heat. Past washaterias, post office, street corners, roadside parks, highway cafés where my people come and go in this heat.

Her name is Ruth. She makes a joke about her ex–old man being "Ruthless."

We turn up the lane to her house, pines arch overhead. She lives alone, she says, pulls hard on the cigarette, fogs my truck, smiles coyly.

We'll take our time, Ruth. We'll have days together. A whole week. Despite this heat, nothing's too good for you.

HOUSTON POLICE ARREST SUSPECT

The Houston Police have located and arrested John Wood Phelps in connection with last month's brutal murder of his ex-wife, Ruth

Mackenzie Phelps of Route 4, Coldridge. Sheriff Johnny Scotts told the paper this was the big break he'd been looking for. "Heaven knows we've got a lot of questions to ask Mr. Phelps," Sheriff Scotts said. Though specific details of the murder have been kept from this community, what has become known has led to some uneasiness in rural households throughout Madrid County.

December 1975

I cried an hour up in my room. And I went out and bought a pint of Canadian Club. I usually never drink when I rent a room in some boardinghouse; I go down and watch TV. It's that time of year and those people show up on the news, don't they? Black kids with chestnut eyes and their fat mothers. Old white men, their hair yellow, their chins all stubble and spikes, sunken cheeks.

Yesterday I drank too but it was only some hearty burgundy. We sat and watched TV. This program where lions circle herds and bring down the weak or lame. Wildebeests standing like huge dumb mountains of flesh. Stupid eyes. Looking here and there but seeing nothing important, missing the details that'd save them. Asking for it. Lions coming close to crouch low, their eyes always moving, chests rattling.

Oh God, I pray, my knees on the stained oval rug by the bed. My elbows deep into the horrible soft mattress that rises around me at night like mud, quicksand. Oh God, I'm sorry I missed the war. Missed serving at all. I love this country of ours. I have a tiny flag I got from a store. It's a pin and I wear it on my shirt collar up above where it buttons down. Always on the left side over my heart.

Protect this nation under God from those stupid people who'd bring it down. Those fat black mothers and old men. From people whose cheap plastic laundry baskets are split, fold flat under their arms. Those noisy cars, smoking blue oil, destroying our air. Bless people in strong houses on clean streets with bright streetlights.

I don't read things. I've never read anything except what's necessary. Street signs. Directions on medicine bottles. On hand dryers: push and rub hands together vigorously. I don't read the Bible. Only those magnetic-letter signs in front of churches. In the beginning was the word. In my Father's house are many mansions.

I love this country. I hate I missed the wars. How about those women who take shopping carts home?

Who do you love? All the other Americans. The astronauts who work where it's clean and clear. The boys in uniform. Mothers whose children are fat, rosy-cheeked, lovable. Thin fathers in suits. People with their own washers and dryers. With new cars.

May everyone get the gifts this year that'll do them some good. That'll save them from the lions.

In my wallet there's a wrinkled bumper sticker. If I owned a car I'd put it on the windshield. "America: Love It or Leave It."

Toward New Year's I get restless, moving from one boardinghouse to another. In Gettysburg, Pennsylvania, I find a wonderful old hardware store. If I'd gone, then gotten the GI Bill, I would own a hardware store. Full of useful things fine people come in to buy to fix drips and torn screen doors. I buy a new ice pick on a card. Still a wooden handle. Still a bargain at $1.29. Someday I'll buy a dozen because you know they'll quit making them soon. Who needs them anymore?

POLICE SEEKING CLUES IN MURDERS
The bodies of two male children, approximately ten and twelve years old, were discovered early yesterday morning by state employees emptying dumpsters at a roadside park on US 250 twenty miles south of Wheeling. State police are questioning residents along US 250 in an attempt to identify the two boys. Details are being withheld pending identification, but sources in the Wheeling Police Department say the two children were bound wrist to ankle and stabbed repeatedly. There is no evidence of sexual molestation.

April 1979

There is rain against the window of my room. Has my life been a dream? I ask my coffee. Do I dream with my eyes open? There's a face in the mirror. It's almost fifty, I think.

I read about black holes in a *Newsweek* I take from the bus station. And I'm one. Everything collapsed, collapsing. Unbelievably heavy with years, thirty years of dead leaves, spring green, Minneapolis, Rock Springs, Detroit, Atlanta. The soldier dressing in the morning, after coffee. All the armor, including righteousness.

I am not crazy, I swear to myself. The boundaries of the country expanding, deteriorating. While I can only contract, suck into myself cities and days, my people, their waste.

The gypsy moth takes one, sweeping down from the sky. The moth doesn't read or write or speak or hear, listen, grow larger, only smaller. My hands shake now; my back's bent. My eyes as milky as theirs at their coldest.

I work even harder. A frenzy of concentration while spring brings other things to America outside. We lost the war. The people have lost their resilience. My people only increase.

The man turns to me in the line and snorts at the service. He's there for food stamps. He fails to notice I don't have a letter in my hand. My hand in my pocket. My smile for him and my country. It's everywhere on posters. Around us the faces of Roosevelt, Stowe, Mencken on stamps.

The child I see left alone in the car. A parking lot full of activity but the black hole edges in invisible. I am invisible. I have always been unseen. I'm not in the mirror some mornings. Sometimes I fail to appear until afternoon, over a sandwich. Through me, in the bathroom, there's a crack in the tile, the calendar from two years ago, the naked hooks behind the door. Brass plate gone sea green. Humidity streaking everything. Surfaces the feel of snake. So many simply go unreported. Missing because I've found them.

Had I gone, come back, sat still, it would all be over. But no GI Bill, no store. I imagine myself a General Grant. As short as he, exaggerated next to Lincoln, that great American. Never out of uniform. I lie on cots in flophouses always dressed.

I take the epaulets off, remove the brocade. Wait at newsstands in the poor sections of the city. They buy a paper. I'm in it. And next to them at the same time. The power of being invisible, two places at once; a dozen places at one time. My hand on the Navy Colt fresh from its paper card.

Roman legionnaires served twenty years. Almost all their short lives. This is a prayer. From a black hole to the things it swallows, absorbs—even the light. Tomorrow let me be absent from Lincoln's side. In this photograph I carefully clipped from a book in the library.

I act. All those others sit and carp. Despise the poor, illegal aliens, welfare, communists, atheists, the poor. Action. Action. Action. McClellan to Hooker to Grant—that black hole in the wilderness. The movement of the horses outside muffled by the canvas of the tent. On the cot I alone hold the entire country in my mind.

"MAFIA MURDERS" ALARMING

Salem, Oregon (UPI) The State Attorney General has called for the formation of a special commission to coordinate the investigations of the so-called "Mafia Murders." The proposed five-person task force will gather information and direct state law enforcement officers in an attempt to capture the murderers who have gone on a rampage the last six weeks throughout western Oregon. So far five victims have been found. All were bound, gagged and shot "execution-style" with one bullet to the head from a .22 caliber pistol.
MORE DETAILS ON OP-ED PAGE AND READERS' LETTERS.

August 1983

I don't know if the street's foggy or my eyesight's getting worse. I got glasses last year but they're no help at all. Every morning this month I've walked along Seawall Boulevard past the Flagship Hotel and the Galvez. It's warm, the air thick and salty.

I walk toward town and, with the usually stiff wind at my back, I come into Mae's Café and have coffee, look out the window.

Those people all around me here, but now I thank God for my lousy vision. I nod at the ugly waitress, elbow a space between two delivery-truck drivers. Smell bacon grease, coffee, the terrifying odor of six o'clock cigarettes.

I tell myself stories all day. The garage in winter. My father's auto-repair shop. He'd be late because he'd still be drunk until nine or ten when Mother'd get enough coffee in him to "start his engine," as she called it.

It is cold, the light through the filthy panes the color of the ashy deposit on spark plug tips. It could be terrifying, I knew. Empty. Greasy. Leaden light. The floor oily. All the surfaces cold. The tools, the destroyed engines. Tailpipes bent in fantastic shapes. But I breathed it all in deeply. Stretched myself on the single stool. The table in front of me cluttered with broken things my father would fix. He could fix anything. Wire this, tighten, solder, wash clean and new with gasoline. I knew I was exceptional too—an eight year old so full of admiration for his father's abilities.

This morning over the black coffee I quit recalling and turn around quickly, squinting hard, which helps me see a bit clearer, farther. I've had this feeling only once before and then it passed. In Tucson at the bus station. I walked all over the place. Feeling it get weaker. My neck hot and prickly, my collar soaked.

He's sitting at the window in a booth. I take my coffee with me, ashamed the cup rattles so loud on the saucer. I sit across from him. He's still looking out at the row of cars facing the window. There's a Polaroid camera on the table by the salt and pepper. He's had a big breakfast, a stub of toast, yellow egg stain on the chipped plate.

When he does look it's only toward me, not at me. My neck

cools. I want to say everything at once. I think of the bumper sticker in my wallet. He drinks his coffee and I follow him, my eyes on his face that nods and smiles, his front teeth gapped. Smiles toward me in recognition. We know one another. The feeling's mutual. We do the same work. He takes a deck of cards from his coat pocket and strips off the rubber band, begins laying them out on the table above his dirty plate. It's a game, I think. But I see they're not cards at all but larger—photographs. I look up but his young face is red with concentration as he separates the pictures into stacks.

He's turning them upright for me. I look at them without touching. Pulling my head back I see the details clearly now. I glance up and around quickly but no one's interested in one man's odd game.

I don't stop his deal; I pay at the register for my coffee and his breakfast, pointing him out to the waitress. Outside I lean over the newspaper rack, my fingers through its cold wire frame, and look through the window. He picks up the stacks and wraps around the rubber band.

Downtown it's either foggier or my eyes are worse as the day wears on. In the city library I hold the *National Geographic* at arm's length.

COMMUNITY STILL GRIEVES

It's been almost three months since our city was racked by the barbarous "Posed Murders" of the Jeffrey Holms family: Jeffrey; his wife, Alice; their two daughters—Kathryn, 5, and Sarah, 10. Many residents of Galveston have written expressing their grief at the senseless loss of one of the city's most successful young businessmen. We can only offer this consolation. The Holms family was deeply committed to our community. Jeff and Alice chaired many civic organizations over their fifteen years here in Galveston. But two stand out—the United Way and the Seamen's Mission. The Holms family lives on in these and other fine organizations and in the hearts of all those the Holmses' special brand of humanity touched. So we must, as difficult as it is, put these dreadful things away and turn from the distrust of our fellowman such cruelty naturally brought out in all of us. It's time to invest our emotions in valuable projects that speak of man's worth. This way the Holms family lives on.

October 1986

I think I've had another stroke. For a long time there were only shadows. Then, later, light and color. Now someone pushes me out into the large filthy room full of windows and them and their noise. So I sit but I don't look around at the others.

I tell myself stories until someone pushes me back, hands hoist me onto the soft damp mattress.

Someone visits. Sits blocking the lower windows and my view of scrub oak, an empty bird's nest between forks of a thin branch.

I think it's the awful young man from the seaside café. But maybe it's only the orderly though this uniform is navy blue, the name tag blinding silver in the light. I wasn't on the coast at the end, before the first rain of light, shadows, noise. But if it's him, I turn away. He's crazy. Such nastiness in those photographs. But moving my head takes a half hour. The field of vision slowly shifting to the left. The others in chairs everywhere. The faces. Dirty gowns. Near my feet a yellow puddle from one of us. I clench my teeth. It takes a half day, toward dark, to do that. Surrounded by them now and powerless. My hands nowhere near Navy Colt or thin brown belt. They just go on and on. Living until they're wheeled back inside too.

I cry. There're hundreds here. Hundreds everywhere. Thousands on the street. Themselves. Their children. But the young man chooses foolishly. And takes terrible pictures.

In the Marine Corps our motto was Semper Fidelis. Always faithful. Semper Fi. I had a bumper sticker that said that once. Always true to my country. But not now. Surrounded by so much to be done. Sitting in their piss and stink. In the middle of this herd. Outside some fool takes his Polaroid from door to door. And then visits me here. No, it's the orderly. But he's new then. Knowing the difficulty of my movements, he sits close, his knees touching mine. He smooths the dirty plaid blanket and deals the cards faceup. It's an old game I've played years ago. Mexican Sweat. Except in his version only I get cards. I moan and he talks more. Brings me water. Holds my head back. The young man deals and deals; all the cards seem to be face cards. The game involves questions. A card, his dark finger pointing, a question. Card, finger, question. But around me there is noise. Outside there's traffic in the street. We don't need this game, I try to tell him but can't. My tongue thick. There is work. Let's work. But someone else to my right starts in with questions. His fingers on the pictures are pink and fat. His coat sleeve navy blue with a white strip. But my jumpsuit's black. My hand on the cold struts, the wind a hundred miles an hour through the stubby wings and then I let go. Out of nowhere. The earth coming up like a dream. From here pastures are green and plowed fields brown. Blue lakes, white straight roads. Nothing ugly yet. Not until I rush down and they rush up and the impact is tremendous.

RISING WATER, WIND-DRIVEN RAIN

August 1687

Pierre Eugene Berthier locked his fingers in the roots along the creek bank and pulled himself up. The two men below stared after him, shading their eyes from the terrible sun. Berthier ignored them; he walked away from the dry creek into the sparse shade of the post oaks. A dozen things might have troubled him, led to another series of desperate pains just below his ribs that would bring a cold sweat underneath the hotter, constant sweat. He scratched his arm covered with the red welts from mosquitoes which swarmed in black droves despite the lack of pools anywhere in the sandy bends of this goddamned nameless creek. "Should we name it, too?" they had joked at first, after they had strangled the bastard farther south on some other, larger creek. Maybe it was wrong to have done it then, as he knelt.

Or Berthier could worry about the Karankawas somewhere along here who ate flesh. Soaking it for two days in tidal pools. "They like their salt," they had once joked. The weapons heavy, the helmets like ovens around their brains. The past an endless series of mistakes and deaths: shipwreck—"push on goddamn you men"—illness, wrong turns—"lazy bastards." The names of saints pouring out of his foul mouth like some priest gone mad. Along this flat, wooded plain no heights to name but dozens of creeks colored by the clay in their banks. Once running blood red, yellow. But now, at best, damp patches of sand quickly shrinking under the long hours of sun.

Pierre Eugene Berthier left them in the creek. Call it St. Berthier, he thought. The creek of St. Jude. He smiled as he walked farther into the post oaks and onto what, in 150 years, would become the Mecham survey and, in 150 years more, lot 51 of Amarilla Creek, "Homes from the low 90s."

There were no garden hoses underfoot, no edge of a porch to sit on. Down below, the two men chewed miserable pieces of tobacco leaf as thin as paper and looked at their hands. No faded Coke cans to pry from the yellow clay, not a single shiny piece of broken glass to snag their eyes.

Berthier sat and then stood again. It was not from a dream, he thought. So somewhere, at sometime, it had happened. He was thirty-seven so there was not all that much to recall. The singing of birds brought it back—the image of a rooster crowing. But there was no sound to it. The bird was red but mottled by the shade of a tree. It stretched its neck, flung wide its wings, and raised its beak skyward.

Must be the product of little food and diminishing portions of water, he thought. But he had recalled it the morning they had decided. He saw it right now as he considered moving them farther from the creek. "The hell with St. Jude's course." He'd move them overland and due east. Sitting, then rising again, he walked down to the men and thanked God for their salvation from the name-spewing madman. He recognized in his heart the rooster's mark on him—whatever, whenever it had been. Always an anxious man, Berthier was less daring than determined. And despite the newly surging pain in his stomach, he felt he must read such a thing with optimism.

In a few minutes he would help them out of the creek and together they would continue listening for savages and the sound of running water, a sound easily hidden by the noises of birds, men, the soughing of the wind in these dwarf trees.

They would cross lot 51, where the contractor would build a

solid two-story house, go bankrupt, and sell it for practically nothing to Evan Fredericks and his wife, Alice Wolff.

No one, back then, walked across lots 50 or 52. No cannibal Indians, Spaniards, Frenchmen. But whatever the rooster meant, it came only once more, when Berthier was eighty-seven, sitting in the sunlight of a doorway near Chartres, the cathedral spire directly before his eyes across a field full of late summer wildflowers. But it came and went with hardly a flicker, the smallest cloud across the sun, a brief shadow somewhere in the flowers. Berthier pursed his lips and took a long drink of water from the clay jug never out of reach. He always smelled ripe from the urine he had to pass so often. It frequently trickled in his pants before he could loosen the buttons. Everyone considered him a thoroughly disgusting and worthless old man.

April 1987

Evan Fredericks had not thought about the rain all day. Instead he had tried to concentrate on his work but had really only fidgeted. At lunch he had stayed inside and reorganized some files, straightened his desk drawers. He knew that eventually he would solve the problems they had passed on to him. He had always been able, with time, to get down to work. But it seemed to take longer and longer and he was just over thirty-seven.

Though rain had been forecast for several days, when he stepped outside the gusting rain surprised him, as did the thought he had just had—almost thirty years to retirement. Jesus, he thought. "Jesus Christ," he muttered, as he forgot to unfurl the umbrella but instead rushed down the steps and around the corner to the parking lot. There the full force of the wind hit, whipping his suit tight against him, the raindrops infrequent but large and with the sting of nettles.

Inside the car Evan caught his breath, let the energy of the coming storm distract him from the problems left spread across his desk on endless computer sheets. A design flaw by some young engineer, he thought, as he started the engine and turned on the wipers. The building emerged sharply from the watery blur. He watched other employees scatter across the lot. Wind-sculpted women's dresses revealed panty lines, pubic bulges.

He turned the radio to his usual station to catch the last of the news, but there was only a steady buzz interrupted by the crackle of lightning. It's off the air, he realized, as he pulled into the slow traffic.

Which slowed even more though the city was only medium-sized; one of the reasons they had taken this job, given the choices, was the city's "driveability," as Alice called it. That and the promotion and leap in salary which provided the security for a down payment. He thought of the house, of Alice there now. Ahead of him, the traffic lights went black and the massive storm stopped brewing overhead and stalled, unleashing rain in solid wind-blown waves.

Evan brushed the windshield with the back of his hand, reached and turned the radio to a country-western station for news bulletins, but the announcer seemed unconcerned though the lightning punctuated a song about whores drinking sangria.

From a nearby car, the traffic now only inching forward toward the dead lights, Evan Fredericks would only be a blur through the downpour. Brushing the window free of fog or daring to roll it down, one would see only the silhouette of a thin man in a damp suit, the green light from the dash not softening the sharp chin and nose but rather somehow compressing them, making him look childlike and a bit ill. A boy, dressed in his father's suit behind the huge wheel, pretending in the driveway. Green from having smoked a piece of cigarette from the ashtray. Moving the wheel a little, hoping to be found out soon. "Evan, what on earth are you doing? We've been looking all over. Your father . . . what's that smell? Evan Fredericks . . ."

Taken from the car, right out of the rain. Angry, loving, sympathetic mother. Straight to his room. A slap on the bottom. A hot bath. The comfort of old quilts from dead aunts.

The man in the car was now at the light. The wipers, on high, slapped the chrome edging of the windshield. Evan pulled across the intersection slowly.

At some time he had convinced himself of everything. At some time he had begun acting the role of Evan Fredericks. But this was not what he told himself now, across the intersection, his eyes on the blur of taillights ahead, his left foot poised just over the brake pedal.

But sometimes he felt all the symptoms. Like earlier today when he doubted his ability for a full eight hours, moving from desk to coffeepot, to files, to phone. But not dialing anyone in the building, or Alice at home. Home and Alice, the two things he would not doubt, could not imagine such doubt as that would take. Though really he did. When he counted back ten years to before their marriage or considered the tumors once inside her like spongy fruit.

Or sitting on the floor in front of the sink, his head even with the plumbing, the water pattering from the plastic pipes. I should be able to do this. I can if I only try harder, if I keep calm. Look what you solved yesterday at work. And the gutters look fine. This, the front door lock next, flashing over the garage.

At night, for years, he waited for something to pull him together. I just have to take my time, he told himself. And not get anxious. Evan Fredericks playing the man in bed next to a woman; the man handy around the house. Playing this man in the car. Waiting to be caught, admonished. Eager to confess and make amends in exchange for love and everything else.

What he dreads would be a list including everything imaginable. He is tricked by events, fooled by something he can not describe, though he knows it is not just himself, but something outside somewhere. It all goes too far back. Only keep the bitterness away. Finally, it is all too unclear, too vague. Like this day of wandering thoughts, the problem clearly before him on printouts, the storm generating outside, and his mind on "heartache," which is as close as he ever came to naming the smallest part of it. "Nostalgia," he had only once called it. But he knew even back then, in the car, the cigarette butt dangling like George Raft's, that the very instant of make-believe threatened him. As if he might not become Evan again, though he was unsure of the severity of the loss.

The man in the car rubbed his eyes. Already it had taken him longer to reach the loop than it usually took him to get home. He wanted to see Alice. Tall, stoop-shouldered, standing in the opened garage with a towel for his wet hair in her hands.

The rain had started along Amarilla Creek at noon. It had just begun to drum on Alice's Honda when she pulled into the garage.

Now she drank a cup of coffee and watched it obscure the backyard and sweep heavily across the porch. The post oaks, always poised to litter the yard given the slightest breeze, had tangled the porch with branches, the green leaves dark waving blotches through the sheet of water pouring down the sliding-glass door.

Alice wiped a swath clear and pressed her forehead to the cool glass. But she couldn't see the creek beyond the chain-link fence.

She wished she had fixed herbal tea. Something to calm her anxiety. A flash of lightning caused her to flinch; she jerked her vulnerable face from the glass and spilled some coffee on her stockings. "Shit," she said, and when the thunder rolled past overhead she wished she had counted "one thousand one, one thousand two," as she had earlier. But she was certain the storm was not moving much now. It was almost directly overhead and immobile. She set the cup down and bent to wipe her toes with a paper napkin. She had never enjoyed storms. Her father had been a cattle rancher, and storms had more likely meant drowned calves than green grass.

Alice Wolff had lied about this afternoon to her classes at Clarion Community College. There they were, ready to begin the final few weeks on their research papers, and she had faltered. Standing in front of them she stared at their faces, most of them adults, and she had let them down. Let herself down. Let Clarion down. Dr. Blocker, the department head.

Alice had sent them to the library with a hurried explanation. The younger ones had brightened up; the adults had looked concerned. "Are you all right, Mrs. Wolff?" Mrs. Vincent, too huge to sit in the small desk any way except sidesaddle, had asked. Alice pitied her but was also appalled at the size of her thighs, the flesh always trembling, quaking as if it were registering the faintest earth tremors.

"It's my husband," Alice had said. "Nothing major. Nothing bad. Just unexpected."

But not unexpected. She had always hated the job. This one only a year old. But all the others, too. By March it was like prison. In the fall, she could bear it until Thanksgiving. When Evan comes home I'll be fine, she told herself.

The next burst of wind seemed to change the pressure in the room. Her eardrums and skin felt it, registered something outside. Alice sat on the couch in the den and watched the silent TV screen. A man cooked in a wok. He was selling woks. Below the edge of his table, the weather warnings ran in a line of gold letters. Flash floods possible. Severe thunderstorms. High winds. The entire viewing area. Stay tuned.

Alice took most of her comfort from Evan. She always had. Before she knew she could not have children. Even earlier, when she first realized he was somehow crippled inside. She had learned not to think much about it all because she depended on him.

She had always relied on others. She had never found out exactly what she wanted to be. Her brothers, all older, had gone to college or into the Air Force or Navy. One was a pilot for TWA, one a computer programmer, the youngest a forest ranger in Oregon. But Alice, always the sister and baby, had never, it seemed to her, had much of a chance. Her mother had been that way, too. For a few minutes Alice remembered her before her death three years ago. Not senility but somehow worse. Unable to do anything alone. Frightened of people at the door, neighbors across the street.

Alice saw herself when she remembered her mother, though she had thought for the longest time—all through college—that her mother was the example driving her on. I can't be that way. What way? she asked herself as the man chopped vegetables more deftly than seemed humanly possible.

She had become a teacher by default. Found herself finished with college and with a graduate degree in English. Someone mentioned teaching. The man she had lived with thought she could teach while she became something else if that's what she wanted. But she had never intended to do anything at all it seemed. And she could organize a class well. She had always been efficient. The brothers had gardened and built fences and despised their father's harsh command and never come home again after high school. She had taken over the ledgers and loved the cattle dotting the hillside and the sunsets beyond the serrated tops of pines. She still missed the house. Her brothers had left her to sell it and divide the money she mailed to them.

Alice had always wanted strength of will. She had been surrounded by determined women at college. But there was her mother as an example. Always quiet and courteous, listening and nodding, she directed Alice's whole existence. Alice knew this about herself. And she believed no one she knew, no people in books, so thoroughly understood themselves. It was her triumph over everything else. Certainly Evan had no such understanding. Or Dr. Blocker at Clarion. Her mother or brothers. The fiery women at college.

She accepted herself. Home, alone, she was anxious. Once, given a new course to teach, she was sick to death. But she had planned it perfectly. Dr. Blocker came to evaluate her and nodded and nodded at what she said to the technical writing students. On the form he checked all the boxes marked excellent.

There were no tornadoes with this storm, so she could relax a bit. And, by the end of April, classes would be over. She would have made it through. And this summer they were going to Italy—their first vacation abroad in ten years of marriage.

As she was about to turn on a lamp in the den—outside it was as dull as dusk—she thought she saw a broad sheet of water rushing through the yard, swirling around the trunks of the post oaks just off the porch.

When Evan drove into their subdivision he was terribly worried. Though all the houses in Amarilla Creek Estates were well off the asphalt roads, hidden by yaupons and post oaks, the storm sewers were flooded and the rushing water threatened to reach his car doors. Today had been trash day, and he had to weave his way through tumbling plastic cans, their contents floating ahead of them.

On Creek View, his street, water covered the road and poured down the slope of his gravel drive. His front yard was flooded. Wiping the windshield, he slowed to a stop and tried to locate a reference—a newly planted bed of lantana, a water faucet at the foot of some yaupon—but couldn't. He realized it had all disappeared under the yellow muddy flow.

Alice had the garage door open. She stood amid the rubble of boxes they hadn't quite gotten to in over a year. They had laughed about what could possibly be in them since they seemed to have everything they needed. Maybe they're somebody else's, he remembered saying.

Evan slammed the door shut and splashed through the water, his head bowed, ready for the towel. But stopping in front of her, he raised his eyes. She had been crying; her face was puffy and seemed old. He hugged her awkwardly, causing them both to totter a little, their legs bumping into boxes. Alice held on; they seemed to dance a bit to gain their balance. She took a deep breath and brought the towel to Evan's face, patted it dry as if he were asleep and she didn't wish to wake him. He closed his eyes and tried to shut himself down a little.

"What'll we do?" Alice asked and, laying the towel on a box, took Evan to the garage door. Looking down, he saw how the water had risen over the lip of the foundation and was slowly gathering itself to menace the nearest box.

"Jesus Christ," Evan said. And for a while they stood there waiting. He felt caught again. The child playacting the adult. Alice was ready to mind. She was ready to wait and listen. She refused to notice his lips moving or to question whatever it was he had never possessed for himself.

The next day the newspaper would be filled with accounts of the localized flooding. Of how, for some reason unclear to meteorologists, the heavy thunderstorms had stalled directly over the city and dropped nine inches of rain in under four hours. Two young boys had already drowned in separate events—one lodged facedown in a storm sewer; the other swept off a raft he had launched down a street—but no one knew this yet. As Evan and Alice didn't know that the rain coming down even harder now would produce real threats to them.

Soon they were working frantically. Evan tried moving the mystery boxes because the water began funneling in from the drive. His mind churned a thousand ragged thoughts as he sloshed around in the cold muddy water. Twigs floated into the garage, pieces of trash from somewhere up the street. It's not fair. It's our first house. Goddammit, stop it *now*. He felt his pulse in his throat. His brain felt as if it were full of clots ready to break loose. I'll die, he thought. I'm about to fall over with a stroke.

Later Alice phoned the police. 911. "What do we do!" she had asked in tears. "Put your furniture up. Take things to the second floor. Leave if you should. Where you are shouldn't get too bad. Some people . . ." Alice slammed down the receiver. She ran upstairs and looked from the study into the backyard. Now it was almost completely dark, but though the lightning had almost died out, the sky was lighted somehow, the low swirling clouds at treetop level. Below she saw the roiling water sweep the porch clear. It took her potted plants, dammed the downstream side with deck furniture.

She came back down to the den's sliding doors to see water

coming through onto the linoleum. Save us, she kept chanting to herself as she lay rolled towels along the door and baseboards. Save us, she chanted, thinking she was asking everyone she knew for help. People from Clarion, her students, her parents' spirits, God, Evan. She worked and imagined the community coming to pack sandbags, form a human chain to place them, bail water, put out fires, make coffee. "Please," she said clearly out loud and surprised herself.

Evan discovered the water bubbling up around the baseboards in the living room. When she came in with the last of the towels, her footprints in the carpet filled with water.

She told him what the police had said. They pulled books from the bottom shelves of bookcases. They unplugged the stereo and television. Very soon they'd have to consider taking the furniture they could lift together upstairs. Alice carried, as far as the landing, a wooden rocker that had belonged to a great-grandfather.

She sat down in the soft circle of light from the chandelier high overhead. All the lights in the house on as if their heat would help dry the water up. "If we lose power," he shouted up at her, "we'll leave, okay?" She looked down the stairs to where a thin film of water, filtered clear by the carpet, flowed to meet the water coming in from the kitchen.

Some minutes later, Evan looked into the garage again. He had closed the automatic door and stuffed some work rags into the crack where the door met the concrete. But now the water bubbled up in long sighs and the rags waved like seaweed in the current.

"Goddammit," he said, and stepped down from the door into ankle-deep water. He worked quickly, putting the boxes up on metal shelves and his workbench. He bent to retrieve things as they floated by: candles, shoes, a purse from some waterlogged boxes already split open. He didn't recognize any of the objects.

All the time his mind seemed out of step with his hands grasping here and there. Lifting up, reaching down again. At one point he tried a foolish idea. He opened the garage door and water poured in; he looked back to see it lap over the doorsill and swirl under the poorly fitted door and into the utility room. Then he took his wide stiff shop broom and tried pushing the water back against itself and into the flooded drive. He strained more forcefully than he had in years. His pulse raced, his tie, which he had forgotten to remove, fluttered over his shoulder. He noticed himself reflected in a storm-door pane propped against a shelf.

But he barely recognized himself engaged in such a silly effort. Instead his mind worked in aspic, in thoughts slow and viscous. He despaired. It was their first house after saving money for years. He fretted for Alice inside; he believed he thought her thoughts for her and cursed such a punishing event. All the day's thoughts came back. And yesterday's too. And soon Evan stopped and wanted to cry out. He was a child trying to do combat only adults were able to comprehend. His heart ached more than it had in years. He wished for safety and comfort. It's not right, he thought, as he dropped the broom and watched it float toward the car in the driveway, its headlights still on. I shouldn't be punished. Or if this is the punishment, get it over with. He wished he had not come home from work. Or gone to a party and met her. He wished he had stayed in Oklahoma. Never undressed her, taken his own clothes off. He told himself he was a crybaby, but the admonition didn't have much of an effect.

He sloshed through the cold water, leaves clinging to his pants legs. He grabbed the broom before it floated around the corner of the house.

He stood up under the eaves with it in his hands and looked around. The low clouds boiled overhead reflecting the city lights. Lightning occasionally ripped the sky. The rain had lessened some. Evan tried to gauge its intensity by holding out a wet arm. All around him the water sucked and moaned. Somewhere far off he heard a shout.

"Hello!" he yelled back through cupped hands. But instead

of a reply, the klaxon of an ambulance or fire engine began in the distance. Stepping off the foundation, he felt the water rise to his knees. He clung to the brick wall like a blind man. Passing shrubs, he noticed the debris snared in their branches. At the rear of the house he stopped. Here the water rose to his waist as the yard dropped sharply to the creek.

Evan felt for the rain again with his bare arm. Then he watched something black and large emerge from the water in front of him. He opened his mouth and called Alice. Down the hill the landscape timbers of the perennial bed showed symmetrical in the twilight. The first thing he had built in his own garage for his own house. The water was going down. "Alice!" he shouted. "Alice, come look!" Yes, he kept thinking. Yes. Yes.

But then the rectangle lost its form, turned away from him. Rotated on its plane. Its shape dissolved and Evan realized he could see none of the plants, not even the top of the tall hollyhock, and he knew the water wasn't going down. Then the floating landscape timbers eased over the farthest corner of the chain-link fence and rushed downstream. The cold water pulling at his thighs had told him the truth all along. But the betrayal wasn't lessened. He retraced his way along the wall even though the swamped porch was closer. He remembered that floods brought out snakes. Back in the garage he looked at the incongruity of yellow flood water illuminated by the overhead light. He listened to the echo of his foolish shouting voice. "Alice, come look. Alice, we're saved."

Some time later Alice went to the garage for help. She had run out of towels, the floor was flooded, and she needed Evan to come back inside. But when she opened the door and saw him sitting on a stool looking out into the car lights, she closed the door quietly. There's nothing to do, she thought.

Alice sloshed across the kitchen linoleum and opened the sliding door. She took in a deep breath of wet air and listened to the rain slashing through the oaks and yaupons. But over that noise and the distant sounds of emergency vehicles she heard the sharp cry of a cat. Stepping out into the rain to the edge of the porch, Alice listened until her eyes adjusted to the odd glow from the low clouds.

The cat clung to the top of the chain-link fence at the side of the house, its feet constantly moving, its balance uncertain in the tangle of trumpet vine. The black water ran easily through the open links but surged around the vines. The fence swayed, the precarious cat cried, its voice almost the sound of a baby's.

"Here, kitty . . . kitty, kitty, kitty." Alice slapped her thighs to attract its attention. And before she spoke again, the cat leapt into the water.

"That's it. Come on," she shouted as, crawling across the porch on her hands and knees, the water over her calves, she edged toward the railing.

"Come on . . . come on over here," she said softly, almost to herself. For a moment the small dark shape of the cat's head disappeared under a swell of water and Alice regretted calling it off the fence. But in a few seconds the slick head emerged. The cat paddled furiously toward her and, when it was within arm's length, she lunged to grab it, falling across the flooded boards.

She sat up, the soaked cat against her soaked chest. For a while it was quiet from its exhaustion but suddenly it pushed vehemently against her chest until she dropped it. She watched it cross the porch and leap up on the railing. After a second's hesitation the cat scaled a tree and disappeared above the roofline. Alice smiled. She closed her eyes and relived the last few minutes. She saw the triangular head barely above the water, the cat swimming furiously against the current. She thought about how much cats hate water. It was something she had never seen before. Both their chests had rattled for a time. She opened her eyes and retraced the cat's escape up into the oaks above Amarilla Creek.

Around ten the rain stopped completely and the water began to fall. By midnight their yard was empty.

They slept with the windows open so they could listen for more rain. The wet carpet and soaked boxes and furniture produced a sour pungent odor.

The next morning they both got up with headaches. Evan phoned the insurance company while Alice washed and dried towels. The water had left its level on the white walls in the living room. The legs of the dining-room table were discolored three inches above the floor.

Evan came into the utility room shaking his head. "Rising water's not covered in this state." He took Alice's coffee cup off a shelf and drank. "Wind-driven rain . . . now that's covered. That's what I should have said. I'm sure that's what she expected me to say . . . wanted me to say." He laughed an ugly snort of a laugh. Alice looked at him and bent back over the clothes. She didn't know what to say.

Angry all day, Evan barked at people over the phone. Around noon two men came and took up the carpets and plugged in huge fans. Evan followed them from room to room telling them this was their first house. Before the men left, they told Alice to run the air-conditioner though it was cool outside. Mildew would ruin the carpet, they said, if she didn't.

The next day they would take a walk around the neighborhood. And Evan would stop and point out the water marks on trees. He would laugh at rising water versus wind-driven rain. They would learn the neighbors had been better and worse off. One had just installed new parquet floors. Then, of course, there were the two drowned children.

But this day, with only drizzle falling out of a nonthreatening, light gray sky, Alice had finished the best she could inside and surveyed the yard. A jumbled carpet of waste paper and twigs covered the grass. One of the wooden flower borders had lodged in a corner of the fence. Broken planks, empty plastic flowerpots, a child's sandbox, two pairs of garden gloves, and a ton of other odds and ends from neighbors upstream were wedged in yaupons, draped around the base of the oaks, caught in the porch railing.

"Shit," she yelled, and hopped to the faucet to wash the biting fire ants off her bare ankles. "Bastards," she said as she danced under the water. The flood had destroyed their beds and they swarmed over everything.

Alice worried about the flowers laid flat by the water. She hoped the sun wouldn't come out suddenly and scald everything.

Back inside she dressed quickly in pants and a long-sleeve shirt. She gently opened the bedroom door and watched Evan under a pile of covers, only the top of his head showing.

"Hey, you going back to sleep?"

Evan moved his legs but didn't turn over.

"Come on, let's clean up outside. I think we can save most of the flowers. Come on, you won't believe the stuff washed up out there. I think there's a tennis racket in the willow over the creek."

She waited, smiling, for Evan to speak. She wanted his help. She pictured them raking up the trash, cursing the ants they'd never considered when they'd decided to move south. She would have liked his direction about the side fence that now leaned downstream at an odd angle. How do we straighten this? What's the plan? You, she thought, are the one with those sorts of ideas.

"Hey, come on." She waited. "I'll be outside. Come on out when you're ready."

But when he did appear, hours later, he only waved and sat on the steps drinking a beer. Alice saw his face and knew that whatever had always been the matter had gotten worse. She smiled at him and waved her rake. "The ants'll eat you alive!"

All afternoon she forayed off the porch to work in a frenzy before the ants forced her to the faucet. She raked up huge piles of trash.

She was ashamed she felt better when Evan walked around to the front. To check out water marks, she thought. She considered the cat in the current and felt warm with embarrassment. It was too silly. It was a sentimental image from Walt

Disney. The cat pawing the dark water. Its teeth bared at the struggle. It could be a poster for a child's room; though probably too frightening. She considered some possible captions: "Just Keeping Your Head Above Water," "Hang In There."

She bent over to slap at the ants covering her tennis shoes. God, Alice, you are a silly girl.

May 2039

The thin old woman stopped to catch her breath, which came in shallow pants fogging the chill air. She set her net bag down and stepped off the narrow road to look first up the hill and then down to the monastery already hidden by the pines. She nodded and smiled in recollection of the monk jabbering away at her. She had bought soap and honey and fingered the lovely carved saints no bigger than the palm of her hand.

"You always speak the best Italian," he had said.

And Alice had quoted the florid passage from some ancient poet that was inscribed over the entrance to the church. It was a ritual between them. Every two weeks for sixteen years.

Alice picked up her bag and crossed the mountain road to the side sloping down toward the river valley. She held on to pine saplings until she reached a level spot behind a large rock. She pulled down her pants and then her panties, the cold air chilling her hips. She peed only a brief burst. Then she wiped with a Kleenex from her pocket and reached forward to hide it under a rock. There was another there already and Alice laughed. She carefully worked her way back up the hill to the road.

She bent to her task, the bag slapping her leg. The monk had asked about her sister who had visited at Christmas. And Alice had laughed and reminded him it was her daughter. They had both enjoyed his transparent deceit.

She walked and tried to breathe deeply. She took in the odor of roasted meats from the roadside restaurant ahead. Farther up the hill she could see the stone fence of the first decrepit hotel that overlooked the Arno valley below. But Alice couldn't forget what had happened earlier. She had risen long before Claudia, their housekeeper. She had made bitter instant coffee, listened at Evan's door, and come out onto the small veranda perched above their yard. Only a sliver of the dull red river showed far below and at a distance of some miles.

Lifting the already lukewarm coffee to her dry lips, she had looked down and seen very clearly the head of a cat, chin down, eyes shut, wet. Paddling furiously. Alice involuntarily closed her own eyes but they saw only the morning light made red, the minute detritus of a night's sleep passing like odd shaped bacteria under her lids.

She had never owned a cat. Allergies, she thought. She had never seen a cat swim. She was surprised by the vividness of detail.

Later, passing through Vallombrosa, walking easily downhill toward the monastery, she had changed direction, marched quickly into a bar where the locals usually waited for the bus down the mountain into Firenze. The old men were smoking and talking about the flood. There were no old women, of course. Some of the men nodded at her. The bartender shook her hand and asked about her husband.

"No, he's the same. Good days and bad days." She ordered a vermouth because it was the first bottle her eyes lighted on. The surprise of the taste so early almost choked her. She had looked at herself in the mirror behind the bottles.

Now Alice crossed the road. "She looks exactly like you. As lovely as they come," the monk had said, complimenting Alice and Elizabeth. She had nodded, thanked him for his kindness.

Today she was not so fearful of sudden traffic, Italian men attacking the curves in small cars. The flood below kept the road deserted. It had for a week now. The old men in the bar read the Milano newspapers aloud to one another. Worst flood in eighty years. The Ufizzi damaged. Damage in the millions. Church frescoes awash and destroyed. They swore, slapped their knees. She had had one more vermouth—this one almost tasteless compared to the first.

The huge redheaded woman who owned the restaurant knew her and seated her in the window in the light. A warmer place for an old woman, Alice thought. She ordered roasted chicken from the spit and a liter of the local white wine. She knew she should go on home and eat something more sensible than the greasy chicken. But instead she took a long drink and smiled, wondering if she were becoming a lush.

Perhaps she and Elizabeth had come to look alike. Mutual osmosis. At Christmas, they had sat near the fireplace. Another warm place for old women.

Elizabeth was an old woman. Sixty-three. The adoption agency had been unsure of her exact birthday, so Alice had chosen November first for no good reason.

"How is he?" Elizabeth had asked in the concerned voice she manufactured only for him, for questions about Evan.

Alice had been thinking about the ten copies of her new book on technical writing Elizabeth had insisted on bringing from Boston. Alice had told her earlier about her latest idea for a book expanding the chapters on grant writing and proposals. But now they talked about Evan, Alice trying not to manufacture any tone at all. She didn't think she was successful.

She chewed the juicy chicken slowly. But she drank the second glass of wine in one long swallow. He should have died long ago, she thought. I am not being cruel; it's the truth. Three heart attacks ago.

Afterward the thin old woman walked up the hill in a bit of a daze. She stopped again and drank one last vermouth, almost deciding she would begin a tradition. She talked loudly with the old men about the flood. She imagined the odd swimming cat again.

It was two o'clock when she climbed the stone steps up from the road to their small house. Her legs ached. Her head was light and seemed pumped full of the cold spring air. Swept clear by breezes.

Alice stood at the edge of the small yard and looked past the serpentine road to the slice of river. The sun had come out a couple of times but had now gone behind dark low clouds threatening a continuation of the past week's deluge.

Finally, the wines neither jumbled things more nor sorted things out. What she had settled on for years was duty, responsibility mixed with moments of pity and devotion—this almost in a religious sense; the closest she came to religion. She sometimes supposed all of this might be love. But she as often doubted that. Now the doctors said the most recent advances in chemical treatment could insure him five or ten more years.

Alice half turned to look up at the house behind her. She had almost forgotten him for some years after they adopted Elizabeth. Consciously and with devotion she had become the child's mother. But he was never the father. It was not the arena he chose. Instead he wrestled great accomplishments from the work he seemed to despise. He kept at it with frightening obstinacy because the pain seemed to provide something of value. This she had reasoned out long ago.

The old woman's mind was full of trick mirrors. And knowing this, she dismissed practically everything that wasn't about the girl or her own work. She knew for certain he had never been cruel to any living thing except himself. He had struggled like some hopeless addict. He had become his only reason to wake up, eat, go to work, have heart attacks, come here to find Santa Maria del Fiore.

Alice turned back to look into the valley. Once she must have hated him or respected him. Maybe, she thought, that's not the right order. Even now she would like to be able to ball it all up into something she might call love. Lately she desired some single word of summation. She was not restless without it, but she thought it couldn't hurt anything.

She wondered if it was God and religion he looked for when, up until last year, he had been able to take the bus almost daily down the mountain to Il Duomo. She saw the sullen face, the bright eyes across a dinner table. It did not seem the face of a pilgrim; but what did she know? Five or ten more years. If he had died with the first heart attack, he would have put his head down on his desk. His hands in his lap. The second and he would have stopped mowing, sat on the damp grass, his legs spread out touching a bed of turk's cap.

Alice imagined the river; brought it up close as if her eyes were some sort of telephoto lens capable of great magnification. And she imagined herself floating downstream and into the city. She drifted through the flooded streets to the beautiful building that housed the Chamber of Commerce. She had scheduled a series of lectures to give on proposal writing. She would translate two chapters from the book Elizabeth had brought and adapt them to the Italian bureaucracy. Then she'd photocopy them and hand them out. She knew exactly what she'd say. She wanted the river to fall quickly and the city to dry out. Now proposals, requests for aid, would be more in order than ever before.

The particulars of the memory never came to him. Only the broadest terms. More an emotion, a passing feeling, than anything visual. It was like those involuntary shudders an aunt or uncle long ago would have explained by saying, "Rabbit ran across my grave."

Evan looked out the window and down at the thin old woman. He watched her idly swing the net bag. Claudia sang somewhere in the house, the melody was low and guttural.

The feeble man wiped his sweaty face with a dish towel he kept in the pocket of his bathrobe. It was the new medicine. It came on like this in the early afternoon and, again, late at night. Soon the towel would be soaked, smelling of ammonia, and he would call Claudia for another. After this bout was over he would bathe, change his clothes, and lie down.

But the effort would be great. The towel remained poised without touching his forehead and cheeks. His skin splotched and oily. Raw from the salty water, from too many baths, the confines of stiff, newly washed clothes.

Instead he crossed the room to his bed but didn't lie down. He stood by the foot of it. Then he stretched out to reach the stuffed chair first with his hands, pulling his tired legs after.

The feeble man considered his body. The joints ached. The sweat poured everywhere, collecting at his waist to puddle at his crotch. The room, no matter the careful cleaning and airing given it by Claudia, smelled of him. He inhaled deeply and paid attention to the overflowing bookcases, the nearby table piled high with drawings by him and others. The walls at both sides of the window were covered with photographs and reproductions of paintings. In some of the photos he could barely make himself out. In all of them there was the massive red-tiled dome of the cathedral.

But this was all he did now. Look at, not examine. He didn't need to. He knew everything there was to know about Santa Maria del Fiore. Il Duomo. Filippo Brunelleschi's church of the dome. Since the beginning he had loved to say that name, Filippo Brunelleschi. And all the other names, too. The more obscure men, stonemasons. Some leaving only the faintest mark on the sandstone, the pietra serena. Serene stone.

Bathed in sweat, snared by aches, the man remembered walking under the dome or up the steep steps to stand on the roof. At some point they gave him free rein. He had sketched it from every angle in his desperately poor hand. They had let him wander the obscure passageways. The rough interior walls hidden in the dark for hundreds of years. The mason's marks. A piece of frayed rope. The hidden holes for block and tackle.

He tried to love it as he first had coming out of a twilit, narrow street and into its presence. And on the best days he could sit for some time not noticing himself soaked and smelling. He was almost the architect.

But eventually he saw it happen from all points of view. It rose slowly in the air and turned just as slowly as if he could hold one of those vast wooden models of it in the Museo dell'Opera in his hands and rotate it. But the loving play of perspective was not there at all. For just as slowly it came apart at its joints.

The cupola ascended higher, the naves slaked off and floated away. Everything in fluid motion and regular and slow—some metronome set on the particular swing of a grandfather's clock.

He no longer cried out so Claudia or his wife rushed in to him. He either sat still or more often rose from the stuffed chair and lay on the bed, pulling the wilted sheet and quilt up to his neck. The feeble man feeling like a child. His emaciated body a boy's body tormented by some sort of flu whose fever explained the drenching sweat.

He recalled that his initial feelings about the cathedral had been unmolested for a while. Before the advent of whatever it was that always acted as some potent distillate ungluing this and that in his life. Leaving the boy ill in his bed, the puzzle spread out on the quilt near his hands, unassembled.

But it was never God, hidden somewhere in the huge sky of the dome, he asked for. It was Filippo Brunelleschi. For only he could gather up the materials from the quilt and piece them together and leave them together for Evan to see until the unsticking came again.

The ill boy closed his eyes. He might stand up in a moment, the sweat gone. He might softly call out to Claudia or his wife and listen to his voice.

The medicine would be improved again. And such advances would keep him alive for twenty years more.

SIGN LANGUAGE

Friday

The 727 turned to the southwest and vanished into the thunderheads of midsummer. Most of his life, he thought, was captive in that thin shell. And as he turned from the window to face the crowded lobby two thoughts occurred. Or rather, one sharp picture and a hideous thought superimposed. There was a bare field, just off a runway—punctuated by curious lights in cages, white-topped fence posts—and a looming huge fragment of a tail section. This, he knew, was one of those lasting TV images, from the Dallas crash of a few years ago. But the second thing was the unpleasant thought; I'm alone.

Halfway across the carpeted area, Charles turned around and walked back to the glass and waited and watched an identical American Airlines plane rise and bank to the south and vanish. He worried after all those strangers and their families.

Back in the traffic, the car radio on, he wondered what he would do for the next three days. And finally, out of the city, the sun setting beyond the green hills north of Nashville, he still hadn't come up with any answers. Though, unwillingly, he acknowledged a second unpleasant thought: He didn't miss them at all. Not Annie or the girls. But of course not, you jackass. He looked at his watch quickly, always a too careful driver. They've only been gone an hour now. Soon they'll be there and he'd still have two hours to drive before he reached the quiet town and empty house.

Some of the guys at work had suggested driving up to St. Louis for a ball game, but Charles had turned down that and all other invitations until someone had nudged him and winked. The secretaries had pursed their lips.

"Batching this weekend, huh? Take-out pizza and beer."

"Sink full of dirty dishes I bet."

Now he wished he'd gone. He hadn't been to a major-league game in years.

A half hour from home he stopped for gas. And, at the register, he turned to the attraction of flashing lights and gaudy, homemade signs over the deli counter. He bought the big basket of fried chicken livers and potato wedges, a Hostess fried apple pie, and root beer.

But out on the road again, the villages and river bridges becoming familiar, he was ashamed of himself. He glanced down at his soft belly and measured its distance from the wheel by turning his hand sideways. Still four fingers away, though he sucked in more deeply than ever. This isn't good, he thought, and swerved off the road, scattering rocks against a roadside dumpster. He ate exactly four more of the greasy livers and hurled the sack and the fizzing A&W can into the overflowing container.

He hadn't driven on the highway after dark in years, and his eyes ached. He cursed other drivers who didn't dim their lights until the last minute and who seemed too close to his side of the road. He thought about all sorts of things, his mind the usual collage of odds and ends. He remembered a movie about a man who went above the Arctic Circle to study wolves; set down alone in the beauty of places where there are no people at all. Different from those Sierra Club calendars of such places. In the movie there was only the man surrounded by wild hearts and shallow, interpreting breaths.

It was almost eleven when Charles came into town. He'd promised Paul he'd come by no matter the hour for one of his famous Manhattans. But instead he drove slowly past their house on Oakridge and smiled guiltily because he saw all of them in front of the opened bay window, their backs to the street, playing some video game. The blue light of TV showed in most of the houses behind drapes and blinds.

He parked behind the pickup. Two vehicles in the driveway and one driver. But he didn't get out immediately, pick up the evening paper, unlock the doors, turn off the porch light Annie'd left on for him. Instead he watched the moths circle the yellow bulb, his mind busy with all the usual tangle, his breath a little shallow. He felt the tightness in his chest which often awakened him, worried him, worried him even more because he hadn't told anyone. Though he was sure it was anxiety, stress from work. His stiff penis pushed at his khaki pants. His breathing reminding him of the moment Molly, the oldest, was born.

After a while he picked up the paper and unlocked the door. But inside, he decided to leave the porch light on. Afraid of the dark? he thought. "Nothing'll get you, you know." He spoke and smiled at what he told the kids when they all came home after a Disney movie or Wendy's.

He walked through all the rooms pulling down windows and closing blinds and curtains. In the girls' room he got on his hands and knees and dislodged a startlingly real doll baby from between the bunk-bed rails and the wall. This was Susan's, the four-year-old's, favorite place to stash things. In the dimness under the bed he confronted a row of carefully arranged animals and dolls. Tigers and bears and the incongruously small Ken and Barbie.

At midnight he shut off the local radio station's classical hour and sat at the kitchen table, his eyes rummaging over familiar things, many of them almost-decrepit wedding gifts. Last week he'd tried rewiring the sixteen-year-old toaster that gladly accepted bread and instantly, in some electrical supernova, produced squares of charcoal. But now there was the new one with the latest options, extra-wide slots for bagels, in the ritzy patina of brushed stainless steel.

Charles listened for a moment to the buzz of his thoughts and heard his concern for aging faucets, failed cabinet locks, proposals due at work, the muddled melody of something by Brahms.

He thought about how he hadn't been this alone in years. He simply couldn't remember when. He recalled from nowhere the picture of a girl named Brandy sitting astride him, her small breasts jiggling in the firelight. From a camping trip in college. He'd considered camping and canoeing a passion then. But now he thought about how elaborate and purposeful it all was. Choosing this item over that. Being superior and particular. The now-embarrassing extolling of nature's virtues. And he'd never gone anywhere alone. There was no solitude, communion, whatever those hip phrases had been. He'd sawed off his toothbrush handle to save space. He'd exaggerated his Cherokee ancestry. There was seduction in tents and canoe bottoms. He saw his own bare ass pumping away, the silver canoe drifting between banks solid with pines and French mulberry.

He wanted something to happen now. He pushed the everyday thoughts away. His life right now was not taken up with his wife, the girls, the office, his blood pressure, taxes, his mother's failing health. For a moment he remembered he'd promised he'd phone her after Annie and the girls left for his brother-in-law's wedding in Miami. Then he snagged himself on Annie's promise to call in the morning before the rehearsal.

"I'm hoping a woman won't answer," she'd laughed. He saw her long, bony face. They rarely kissed, though they made love often and ferociously. She turned her ass up now and he came at her from behind, their only contact the wetness of groin and buttocks.

Charles took a long, hot bath until his toes and fingers wrinkled. He kept adding the precious steaming water until it was completely gone. He washed his legs and feet; he never got below his knees when he showered. He dozed off in the water and came back in a chill, his watch on the top of the toilet tank fogged on the inside. The cold water raised gooseflesh.

In the bedroom he turned back the covers then went and locked the bedroom door. He turned off the lights and lay still.

But what did he want to happen now? Something unusual, he answered himself. Something wonderful and strange. Something from a pleasant dream or exotic movie. Or maybe not even pleasant. But mysterious. He was sure such things must happen to other people. Isn't that what shows in some eyes? Or were those rich people, celebrities on TV, and was that just money and drugs?

He put his fingers to his forehead. He wondered if Annie had ever had such a thing happen. She seemed light on her feet. "Happy," he said aloud in the dark room, the edges of the blinds rosy from the streetlight at the corner. But I'm fine there, too. It wasn't happiness. That took place in tents, in canoes, at Molly's birth, the placenta like some heavy wet scroll rolled up tightly.

Hush, he told himself. Listen. What is there to happen? And it wouldn't just happen by itself.

Charles got up in the dark and straightened the covers. He took some blankets out of the closet and walked to the brick patio. Outside the sky was clear; he had never really learned the constellations, though once, long ago, he'd gone out at his parents' every night with a star chart and a flashlight. But hadn't that ended up in a tangle of opened clothes and elbows? Or maybe it'd been too hard or he'd lost interest with no one to impress.

He made a pallet behind the row of potted, blooming vincas and leaned against the rail, watching the motionless shadows. A dog barked twice. The hedge at the back of the yard needed trimming. Charles lay down and covered up. A gust of warm wind rattled the bamboo chimes; the sound the clatter of bones.

His head was full of movies and work and images of girls and women and the girls as women, their narrow hard butts now wide and embarrassing. Elvis, the family cat, came up the steps, curious at the strange sight. He put his gray face up to Charles's, and Charles took him into the bed. He'd never slept with a cat before, or with a dog. For a long time they both fidgeted.

Saturday

The third time Charles awoke he swung his legs off the couch and sat up stiffly, aching in a dozen places. He rubbed his eyes and noticed he'd left the muted TV on, which now showed some children's cartoon with animal-people, in ugly colors, locked in dreadful combat.

Tasting his own sour breath, he saw it was almost one o'clock. He wondered when he'd pulled the den drapes closed. Rising, he turned off the TV, opened the heavy drapes, the bright summer light rebounding off the bricks of the patio, needling his tired eyes.

He poured himself a cup of coffee from the pot he'd made at daylight after the neighbors' whispering had first wakened him. Sitting rigidly over the cup in the dainty, cheerful breakfast nook where he'd always felt too large and clumsy, he winced in embarrassment.

"Shhh . . . come look. See him? Over there on the patio. See?"

"Good lord. You think he's okay?"

Charles had barely opened his eyes, his face wet with dew, cat hairs on his tongue and lips.

"Maybe it's a heart attack."

"Maybe Annie kicked him out or something."

They had both laughed like naughty children.

Charles had realized he was the topic of the Hallistons' conversation, the whispered voices as faint as the early morning light. But already the temperature was in the eighties, and though he wanted to lie still until Sam and Karen left the low hedge twenty feet beyond his head, he was terribly hot and miserable. Finally, their whispers lower now, more conspiratorial, he hurried them by groaning theatrically and tossing this way and that. Then he listened carefully over the sound of early mowers and the clink-clink of sprinklers until he heard their patio door open and close. Charles tried to sit but couldn't, his spine a complicated network of aches. He had to turn gingerly onto his stomach and work himself to his knees by using the outdoor furniture until he sat, breathing shallowly, under the shade of the pastel-striped table umbrella.

"Jesus Christ." He pulled a damp sheet over his twisted boxer shorts. He'd popped two buttons off his pajama tops. He'd kicked out in the night and overturned two pots crowded with the white stars of vincas. The black dirt had been taken up into the bedding and his legs were streaked with the grime. Charles shook his head and began cleaning up. He scooped the dirt into the pots and gathered the bedclothes. It was full daylight before he finished and realized he was soaking with sweat and still outside in his underwear. Elvis sat on the steps down to the yard and stared at Charles, who, passing by, gently pushed him off the terrace.

The second time he'd awakened, he'd been asleep on the couch. It was nine by the VCR when Annie phoned. His mind had been full of retreating dreams, the voices of the Hallistons in the hedge, mortal embarrassment.

"Good morning, sleepyhead."

And she'd talked on in her level voice full of straightforward information. Good descriptive details of their flight, her parents' health, the progress of the wedding. He'd talked to the girls, their own voices full of cheer, the sound of birds, of innocent animals celebrating without any heaviness at all.

Now it was afternoon and Charles went to the kitchen and poured out the bitter, hours-old coffee. What foolishness, he thought. "Silly bastard." His concerns now including the patio business, Sam's and Karen's voices, the tone of his wife on the phone. Her voice like a stalactite, fifteen years of accumulation. Steady in the face of operations, death, weddings, pain, and disappointment.

Make me like her, he thought, and was surprised because he had thought he was almost exactly like her already. Aren't I? Isn't that why we married, live together?

The rest of the day he worked hard at all the tasks he should already have done. He hosed down the brick walk and the front porch. He touched up the faded picnic table. He waved brazenly at the Hallistons as they left for the tennis courts.

So I'm alone for a day and I come unglued, huh? He laughed at himself and shook his head at the whole vague idea of something wonderful and exotic. That's the movies talking, not me. And, for the longest time, he considered the devilish power of movies and rock music and commercials over our lives as he trimmed a hedge, even combed out the cat's gray, shedding hair, its desperate claws scratching at the bricks.

But it must have been darkness, twilight, the end of activity, that brought last night back again over all those objections of neighbors, Annie, the kids, misplaced currycombs, slices of cucumber from the Tupperware bowl in the bottom of the fridge. Bob Davis not carrying his weight at work. Hadn't for almost a year now.

Instead of showering, Charles took another hot bath. Gradually unclenching his muscles, the water worked on his mind, too. Looking up and over the lavatory, he saw the sky in its last dark blue light after the first star has appeared but not the rest.

He knew he'd only been deadening his mind, keeping it away, paying penance, too—all at the same time—for some vague desire.

"I'm going crazy, is that it?" Charles's voice ruffled the surface of the cloudy, steaming water.

He knew he'd wasted the entire day. There was tomorrow and then, on Monday, he'd leave work early to drive back down to Nashville.

So at dusk, the stars all out now, he brushed a dried piece of chicken liver off the car seat and backed out of the driveway.

It's not at home; he knew that. What's not at home? He shook his head and drove past the office, the homes of friends.

Turning off Bledsoe onto Poplar, he slowed down as he passed Melanie Kirk's house. At the empty four-way stop he put the transmission in park and stuck his head out the window to look back. Her kitchen light was on. He ducked back in when he realized she was right there in the shadows watering the lawn. Her face, arms, legs, all pale in the dark up under the maples, catching the light from the street lamp directly over his flushed face.

What is this? He drove on, quickly, his foot pushing hard on the accelerator, going faster than he'd driven in twenty years. Speeding down streets crowded with homes, people in their yards, children he saw at ballet lessons, parents he recognized from soccer, piano. So once, years ago, she'd come up behind him at some party—Christmas, Halloween, or, back then, they had parties for no good reason at all. Where had they lived then? Over on Childress, before the oldest was born? Or was it even at their house at all? Charles was bent over the sink, twisting at an ice tray, and she'd fit her body snugly against his, run her fingernails down his spine. And he'd jerked around, popping ice cubes all over the place. They'd laughed, picked them up, talked too forcefully, not looking into each other's eyes.

That was years ago. Before Nick Kirk's second and last heart attack. Nick was small-boned and handsome. And though they were only casual acquaintances who played awful golf twice or three times a year, Charles had liked Nick. And now, oddly enough, missed him after neglecting his memory for ten years. Nick Kirk, who lived very carefully after the first heart attack. He had grown even thinner, more sunken-chested, but somehow that had only increased his handsomeness. He was thirty-two and had gone to bed without complaint and not gotten up.

Outside town, south on Antietam Road, he gathered speed. The car floated around the curves. Charles concentrated on the road. He moved the red needle past seventy. The tires squealed. He drifted over the twin yellow stripes. A blur of a sedan honked at him. The Buick brushed the high grass just off the shoulder.

He sped all the way to Madison County and the river. There at the Minit Market he filled the car with super unleaded and, sitting on the curb, drank a beer from a paper sack. He listened to the tick of the cooling engine. There were other roads in his head. He'd wanted a Mustang 289 for graduation.

"Then what the fuck do you want? What the Jesus fuck will get you to?"

Charles looked over his shoulder past the ice locker to the man on the pay phone. He paced between the rusted-out hood of a lime-green Gremlin and the minute privacy booth, the short silver cord limiting his range. Charles saw the pile of cigarette butts at his feet. He snuffed one out on the plastic side of the booth, the black pockmarks like bullet holes.

"Oh just hold that shit right there. Hell no I didn't. Not for a minute, you hear me? Goddamn right. Absolutely right. Well, so he's a motherfucker, too. You tell him that for me. Coming right from me. Go, tell him. Right now."

"Just fuck you too!"

The young man slammed down the receiver and stood a minute. Then, lighting another cigarette, he put in a quarter and dialed.

"So, we have to talk, right? Am I right?"

At home Charles loaded in the videocassette and pushed the fast forward until the image became what he expected. He turned the sound off and lay on the couch.

No one knew him in Madisonville. He'd just walked right into the adults-only section and picked a number off the rack on the wall. Number 58. He hadn't flipped through the catalogs on the shelf.

He hadn't seen the title. And now he watched something he'd never seen before. Long tongues and penises as thick as beer sausages. The reds and pinks of women's genitalia. All the semen spent on backs and breasts. On opened lips. Lapping tongues. Charles had never had a woman take him in her mouth. And every single moment of sex, even then, in tents, canoes, cars at drive-ins done without such detail, without really looking.

Standing, his penis bulging in his pants, Charles went from window to window, lowering blinds, drawing drapes.

His eyes locked on the large screen that had shown him,

Annie, the girls, *Swiss Family Robinson*, *The Sound of Music*. He felt a tremendous guilt.

Later he lay on the bed and masturbated—something he hadn't done in years. It was awkward, unnatural for him. Turning the light on in the bathroom, washing his hands and stomach, he felt caught. Before he went back to bed he rewound the tape and snapped the box shut. He'd mail it back to the store; he'd use the book mailer they'd gotten the latest Book-of-the-Month Club offering in, just last week.

Sunday

The morning began cool, but by eleven it was cloudy and humid. Charles's aftershave remained sticky, his wet hair soured slowly as he sweated in front of the TV. He finally got up and turned the air-conditioner down to sixty. He watched "Face the Nation" and "Meet the Press." He tried keeping his attention focused on this week's familiar faces. The country had discovered the poor again.

Often he looked out the window at the sky. He considered mowing now that he'd trimmed the hedges. Balancing everything out. Finally, a weed-whacker trim at the base of the flowerbeds, the swingset.

Charles grew despondent. He wasn't, he knew, the sort of person who dwells on things, who takes something and probes it, picks it to death. But in twenty-four hours he'd leave work and drive to Nashville and, by late tomorrow, the house would be filled with them again. The girls arguing like magpies; Annie making lists, catching him up on her family and the wedding. He lay back on the couch and tried his best to take comfort from those scenes sure to happen. He heard their voices and footsteps and his chest seemed difficult to lift, his breath shallow. He sat up.

Perhaps he should have gone to church; it would have helped pass the time.

He watched the Cubs lose until almost six, then he sacked the fridge for sandwich materials. Again in front of the television but looking out at the sky, he felt the same. "I really am going nuts, huh? Is that it?" He remembered a movie he'd seen years ago. In the very last scene Gene Hackman has gone nuts and, looking for a hidden microphone, had destroyed his beautiful apartment room by room. Stripped the wallpaper, pulled up the thin slats of oak flooring. Finally sat and played his saxophone in the middle of it all.

Charles turned off the TV and dressed in his yard clothes. But once outside he couldn't find pleasure anywhere. He mowed a strip from front to back but the grass was so short it barely showed. His mind seemed locked up tight by nothing at all. The mugginess drenched him and his damp underwear chafed. There was nothing unexplained, exotic, mysterious. Only the Sears mower belching, acting up. The Hallistons' terrible poodle barking.

Charles stopped the mower and drove off in the pickup. This time he drove slowly, carefully, through the neighborhoods. He chose streets he liked. He looked at the huge, tree-covered lots, the tremendous houses at the apex of circular drives. Then there were the narrower streets and smaller lots but older, too, with a more luxurious growth of lawns, trees, shrubs.

He drove all the way through town and out toward Mt. Carmel to the south. Five miles out he pulled off into an empty gravel parking lot. Here some huge international company had built and maintained a nature trail which looped through the hilly, forested countryside for two miles or so. It was a payback for a hundred years of corporate robbery. He and Annie had brought the girls out once and made it a quarter of the way around before insects and tired feet had turned them back. Charles shrugged his shoulders and locked the pickup. His sweat had left the dark outline of his back and legs on the upholstery.

He walked leisurely on the trail of pulverized wood bark.

Every so often he stopped and read the slanting red metal plaques and stared off into the deep woods, his eyes searching hopelessly for certain types of maple, oak, ash. He remembered his silly canoeing trips, the dappled sunlight on bare flesh.

At plaque number twenty-seven Charles just stepped off the trail and walked down the hillside, crossed a dry stream, the water in its pools stagnant, covered with a hairy scum, and pulled his bulk through the thicket of undergrowth. He had scared himself already, and each step was taken with dread. Charlie, he kept saying to himself. Charlie, what are you doing? You idiot, the sun's going down. My God, man, turn around. You're not that teenage trailblazer. His thoughts kept hammering in his head trying to stop him, drag him back to the pickup. But after a while he'd sweated them away, and by sunset he only considered his raw thighs and heavy calves.

He walked a full hour, until almost dark, before he knew he could stop and rest without turning back, without running headlong toward the loop of trail and the pickup in the gravel lot. Because by now, with all the twisting and turning up easy valleys—treacherous slopes and limestone ledges soon proved too thwarting—he was lost. The sun was down, the clouds heavier than this morning.

He was tired. He figured he'd sweated away a couple of pounds. He pulled his soaking shirt away from his chest and stomach and looked around at the woods. The light was failing rapidly now. And all of this was incomprehensible. His back and legs began to stiffen; he stood clutching the trunk of a tree and walked on, amazed at the depth of these woods. He'd thought this countryside mostly open and cleared. Where farmers raised corn and soybeans, hogs and dairy herds.

In the dark, the travel was difficult. He learned to move carefully, to judge the distances of dark, unfamiliar shapes, to plant his feet cautiously, aware of the unevenness of the ground. He had fallen a half-dozen times and no longer feared falling, though by moving slowly he only stumbled occasionally, usually catching himself on a low bush or thick, supportive branch.

He feared snakes, animals that shuffled away in the absolute dark of the lowest brush and fallen tree trunks. There was rain high over his head in the treetops; he heard it but it never reached his hot face.

He thought about Annie eating at her brother's dining table. Later, birdsong, harsh and hesitant, broke out all around him.

Suddenly he stepped out of the woods and onto a dirt road that bordered an open field. The dark shape of a cow lumbered past on the other side of a rail fence. He smelled it, heard it defecate. To his left a few hundred yards was a large white frame house up under some trees. Charles blinked his eyes in what seemed intense light after the darkness of the forest.

He turned up the road. The windshield of an old car caught the light from a high window. He heard animals move easily as he passed the barn. Turning his watch face to the sky he tried to tell the time but couldn't.

Almost at the front gate of the chain-link fence he stopped as a pack of small dogs tore out from under the house and raised an alarming racket of yelps and snapping teeth. The bravest lunged against the fence. Charles stepped back, gauging the height to the top bar.

Then a yellow porch light came on and the front door opened.

"Jasper, Mary, shut up, you hear me! Get quiet."

Charles watched the thin old man descend the cement steps, his hand gripping the metal bannister. He scattered the dogs with a swipe of the cane in his free hand. Behind him, in the doorway, a small old woman pulled her quilted housecoat shut and locked it with clenched fists.

The old man hobbled to the gate and caught the top of it. Charles saw the scrollwork that framed a large letter W at its center.

"What the hell can I do for you? Sorta late to be making a social call, ain't it, young fella?"

Charles stepped up to the gate and smiled.

"By God, you're a mess." The old man examined him. Charles

noticed he tightened the grip on his cane, took half a step back toward the house.

Charles waved his right hand in front of his face, dismissed his appearance, any threat he might present. But then, before he said a word, he moved his hands again, the way he'd seen it done in the movies, on TV during congressional hearings. The woman signing at a frantic pace to keep up. Charles hoped they didn't know any better, that they didn't have a deaf son or granddaughter. He took the chance; he had no idea what the odds were. He just knew he didn't want to say anything now. He had no desire to talk. He was amazed at himself; he felt his mouth open, his chin drop. But he moved his fingers in front of his chest slowly, trying hard to duplicate what he'd only half-noticed, hoping to hell this old man and woman didn't recognize the fraud, scream, do anything but let him up on the porch and inside. He considered the news on TV, in newspapers, what his own reaction would be. Dreaded the scream, felt an answering one at the back of his throat.

"My God . . . well I'll be goddamned." The old man spoke over his shoulder. "Livy, he can't talk. It's all with his hands. I'll be damned."

Charles smiled, tried to look harmless, bobbed his head, felt himself act foolish. Livy stepped down to the gate. In the weak light from the porch, her face was the color of her gray hair, which was long and thick and had fallen loose from her nest of pins. It covered her left cheek and one dark eye.

"Can you hear?" she asked. "Can you hear me?"

Charles tried not to blink. He felt himself drifting into some stereotype. The village idiot.

"Deaf and dumb," the old man muttered. "And lost to boot. I'll just be goddamned. Middle of the night. Look at the shape he's in."

Charles caught himself; he'd almost followed the old man's eyes down to his torn pants.

"Mute," Livy said, lifting the gate latch. "It's mute, not dumb, Gale."

She patted Charles's shoulder and brought him through the gate. The pack of dogs came out to sniff his pants legs. Livy ignored them, waded through, pulling Charles with her.

"I don't know about this, Livy." The old man was behind and below them on the steps. "Middle of the goddamned night. No car. Torn clothes. Could be an escaped convict from up at Madisonville. Livy, you hear me?"

They all stopped under the yellow porch light and Charles didn't have any idea what would happen next. He expected the old man to scream in his ear, the sudden trick in those war movies where the spy reflexively turns around and is carried away by the Gestapo. So, you can hear, you swine.

Livy looked into his face. Charles swallowed and smiled his best smile. He signed some more, caught her eyes with his fingers and tried to work them deftly, methodically, in some repeated patterns. He thought behind them, tried to speak with them, tried to tell this beautiful old woman everything he could about his life. What had happened to him, without excuses. What he understood and didn't understand.

"He's okay." She spoke distinctly as if that would enable Charles to hear. "Let's get in out of the mosquitoes."

The old man sat in a chair by the refrigerator and crossed his hands on the cane handle. Charles smiled and ducked his head. The old man nodded his own but didn't move his thin lips a fraction.

She touched Charles's shoulder. "Here," she said loudly. "Here's some supper."

"He's a goddamned mess, Livy. Needs to wash up," Gale added sharply.

Gale hobbled ahead of Charles back through the living room full of heavy ancient furniture. The nap of the horsehair sofa was prickly under Charles's hand. Despite the warmth of the night, a low blue flame burned in the huge gas heater. A tin can of water bubbled in front of the red grates, humidifying the already damp, thick air.

Charles closed the bathroom door behind him, heard the old

man's cane bumping back down the hall. He smelled the soap, the odor of honeysuckle, and washed his hands and face. He opened their metal medicine cabinet and took out the plastic bottles. There were more for her than him. For pain, two a day. Something for blood pressure. For cloudy vision.

He squatted by the tub. It was large, solid, up off the floor on lion's paws that had once been gilded but now had only flecks of gold between the claws. There was the smell of other, unknown lives, and he inhaled deeply. Vicks VapoRub, Ben-Gay, lotions, the funk of hidden, dirty clothes, old furniture, older flesh.

Later he ate two bowls of thick beef stew. The talked about him, wondered all sorts of things. Until, finally, Livy stood and said "Ah ha," and took a pencil stub and notepad from a drawer.

As the two stood close over his shoulder, he breathed in their smells. Gale leaned over as Charles wrote, rested a hand on Charles's shoulder.

He wrote his real name and how he was coming from Madisonville and had had car trouble, walked into the woods, and gotten lost. Then he'd come out here, in their meadow.

"Didn't know they let 'em drive like that," Gale mumbled.

Charles winced slightly for he didn't know either. Then she took the dull pencil and wrote their names, how it was almost midnight and he'd sleep here, they'd take him into town for a mechanic in the morning. Did he need anything else before bed? Anything special? Was he still hungry?

They wrote back and forth for quite a time. Tore off pages, Livy finding another partial pad, Gale sharpening the pencil with a penknife.

Later Charles got into bed, the soft mattress swallowing him a bit. The weak bedside light dully illuminated the room. Charles guessed it had belonged to a child. Who would be much older than he now. It was full of heavy, dark furniture, all topped with lacework and photographs. Most were black and white.

Tonight he lived with these two old people, would sleep in a room unslept in in years, protected by all those small dogs.

He listened to them talking about him. They were almost deaf and shouted at one another.

"Ain't it something. I mean, goddamn, ain't it something."

"It's amazing."

Charles guessed she had a smile on her face. They had done well. Here was something amazing, mysterious, they'd remember the rest of their lives. They'd talk about it, smile, and shake their heads.